MW01603069

Therese Park came to the U.S. in October of 1966 to perform with the Kansas City Philharmonic (now the Kansas City Symphony) in its cello section. After 30 years, she retired and began writing fulltime. Her first novel *A Gift of the Emperor* (published by Spinsters Ink, 1997) deals with Korean sex slaves, mostly schoolgirls, including Soon-ah, the heroin of her novel, forced into military prostitution by the Japanese military during WWII while Japan ruled most of Asia and the Pacific. Park was a featured author at three national bookfairs in 1998—the LA Bookfair, Miami Bookfair, and Heartland Bookfair.

Park's second novel *When a Rooster Crows at Night: A Child's Experience of the Korean War* (iUniverse 2004) is based on Park's own experience as a child living through the horror of the three-year war (1950–1953), which, in a real sense, has never ended.

Her third book *The Northern Wind: Forced Journey to North Korea* (iUniverse 2012) is told by an 18-year-old war orphan working with a group named 'Hope Community' that helped the islanders with the government's New-Village Movement on a South Korean island. One day, she accidentally stumbles across a battalion of disguised North Korean commandos in a remote area, and reports to the group commander. She becomes a South Korean spy and leaves for North Korea, with a mission to accomplish.

In 2006, Park wrote *Midwest Voices* columns for The Kansas City Star-Opinion Page, and between 2009 and 2016, she wrote columns for the Star-Johnson County Neighborhood News.

She is a mother of three daughters and a grandmother of four grandchildren born in the U.S.

To all Korean infants born of unwed mothers or lost children, who lived in orphanages before they were adopted by foreigners, mostly American couples, and forced to leave their 'homes'. While many became successful adults in their adopted countries, some were mistreated.

To all unwed Korean mothers whose countrymen demanded female purity, chastity, and abstinence before marriage, leaving them with no choice but to give up their 'unwanted' offspring and banish them, never to see them again.

To all adoptive parents, who opened their arms and hearts to their adopted children, regardless of their origin and cultural limitations, and raised them with love and dedication.

Therese Park

RETURNED AND REBORN: A TALE OF A KOREAN ORPHAN BOY

Dave & Tracy,

Hope that you'd enjoy this book and get familiar with those who were sent away from their own country —

Therese Park

AUSTIN MACAULEY PUBLISHERS™

LONDON • CAMBRIDGE • NEW YORK • SHARJAH

Ordering Information:
Quantity sales: special discounts are available on quantity purchases by corporations, associations, and others. For details, contact the publisher at the address below.

Publisher's Cataloguing-in-Publication data
Park, Therese
Returned and Reborn: A Tail of a Korean Orphan Boy

ISBN 9781643780238 (Paperback)
ISBN 9781643780245 (Hardback)
ISBN 9781643780252 (Kindle e-book)
ISBN 9781645366676 (ePub e-book)

Library of Congress Control Number: 2019934633

The main category of the book — Fiction / Asian American

www.austinmacauley.com/us

First Published (2019)
Austin Macauley Publishers LLC
40 Wall Street, 28th Floor
New York, NY 10005
USA

mail-usa@austinmacauley.com
+1 (646) 5125767

Foreword

A writer finds his or her story subject from people or events that moved them deeply. As children living in Pusan during the Korean War (1950–1953), my siblings and I visited the orphanage operated by our own parish church many times, thanks to our mother, each time with food or fruit that the orphanage never had enough. Our mother's intention was to educate her children about the war, what it had done to children—some abandoned by their parents or were separated from them in chaotic situations. I was heartbroken at seeing children my age, or younger, who were mostly skin and bones; some so sick they didn't seem to know they were even alive.

As a U.S. citizen for more than a half century, I was shocked when I learned how many Korean children were adopted to childless couples around the world, mostly to the United States, since the Korean War ended in 1953. I actually met several Korean Americans, men and women, who revealed their Korean roots to me. One of them, whom I interviewed and wrote about, showed anger when I asked if he wanted to go back to his motherland but expressed deep gratitude toward his American parents and credited for who he was.

I'm also privileged to have known six American Jesuit priests who established the first Catholic college in Seoul in the early 1960s. They were our dinner guests many times, during which they taught us English and gave us a taste of America, and we taught them about the Korean culture and commonly used idioms and slang. That college turned into a university decades ago that has grown into one of the most respected Christian adult education centers for both men and women in Asia today.

I have a profound respect towards these American Jesuit Fathers for their pioneer spirits as well as their devotion as the followers of Christ.

I hope readers find the story compelling and be sympathetic with the storytellers.

Part One

Chapter One
A Letter from a Stranger

Seoul, Korea, October 2002.

Michael Hamil, 25, looked at the folded white paper his buddy Charlie Knox, a clarinetist with walnut skin, had just handed him as the two men headed to the dressing room down the hallway. The six-member band *The Returned*—made entirely of half-Korean, half-Americans who had been adopted by American families as toddlers but returned to their motherland as adults—had just finished their weekly Friday night performance at the New Age Theater in Yongsan District.

"What's this?" Michael asked Charlie.

"An American priest asked me to give it to you backstage a minute ago."

"*An American priest*?"

"Yep! He was tall and looked dignified, with white hair and a bald spot on the top of his head. He reminded me of Hemingway in photos I've seen."

"Why didn't he give it to me himself?"

"You were busy talking to that cute chick with a boy's haircut. Remember?"

"*Hmm...* I don't know any priest who might want to leave me a note, American or Korean. I'm not Catholic."

"He must know you somehow. Open the note and read it."

Charlie was a year older than Michael. The two met during the *Adoptee Home Visit Program*, a ten-day event three years ago, here in Seoul, hosted by international adoption agencies and the South Korean government. The purpose was to give young Korean adoptees a chance to visit their motherland and learn her history and culture with no cost to them. *The Home Visit Program* included a ten-day stay in a five-star hotel where they attended classes during the day that included watching

11

educational films about South Korea's recent history. In the evenings, a dozen Korean folk musicians and dancers in their colorful traditional dresses entertained them.

Michael and Charlie bonded like two brothers after the orientation. Whenever they were together, they talked. They were both infatuated by music, since they both played in a band. Charlie, a half-Korean, half-Black American, played in a bar every weekend in a predominantly black community in northwestern Chicago, while Michael played guitar and sang, for fun, with a few friends in a suburb of Austin, Texas, mostly at a park on weekends or in a private home. After the ten-day *Home Revisit Program* ended, Charlie and Michael each returned to their homes—Charlie to Chicago and Michael to Austin.

But their friendship didn't end there. They corresponded through emails, sometimes on the phone. One summer evening, Michael learned of Charlie's fear of death when he called and talked about a drive-by shooting that killed two of his friends earlier that day. "Death is no big news here in this neighborhood," Charlie said on the phone, his voice dark and subdued. "The two guys were sitting and smoking on their porch two houses south of me, when gunfire from a moving car killed them both instantly."

All Michael could say was, "I'm so sorry…"

"The sad thing is that we blacks were persecuted by whites long and hard since an ancient time ago, but these days, blacks are killing blacks. Isn't it sickening? Our enemies are not whites; they're our own kind. Hey, Michael, have you thought about going back to Seoul someday? I don't think there are hardly any blacks in Korea. I wanna get away from here, an all-black neighborhood!"

Two years later, they found each other in Seoul again, this time, to make music together.

* * *

The dressing room was lit with white florescent ceiling lights. Tall and wide mirrors on the wall made the narrow room twice as wide. In a chair before the mirror, Michael opened the letter Charlie had given him, the letter that had supposedly been delivered by a white American priest, while Charlie stood next to him and looked on.

Dear Michael,

I enjoyed your concert. Your band touched your audience with its unique charm and compelling stories. I was particularly touched by your number, 'My name is Orphan'. You've courageously told the whole story of your birth and life journey as an orphan, including your graceless childhood on a Texas farm and why you returned to your motherland, all in one song with poetical verses.

Let me introduce myself: I'm Father Patrick Anderson, a Catholic priest who knew your father, Father John Dolan, well. In fact, your father was my mentor when I was in seminary, and later, he and I worked together as spiritual brothers and colleagues at Sonam College, the first Catholic college for both men and women in Korean history, which your father had established in 1961. I taught philosophy for seven years, between 1965–1972. As you might already know, your father passed away a quarter of a century ago, probably while you were in Texas. It was shortly after the Vietnam War ended; and I learned the news of his passing in Milwaukee as a prison chaplain. (God willing, someday I'll tell you why I returned to the States against my will.) I now live here, near Seoul. I want to meet you and get to know you. Please contact me at Sochun Catholic Church, Sochun City, Gyeonggi Province. (Tel: 82-674-6866)

May the Lord be with you and give you peace,
Father Patrick Anderson.

Michael felt the blood rushing to his head. He knew nothing about his father except for what he had read in the note his birth mother had written; the note that had come with him to his new home in Texas when he was four years old saying that his father was 'a very important man doing important things for the Korean people'. The note had been inside a manila envelope—along with his passport and birth certificate, which only showed his mother's name as a single parent.

"What does it say?" Charlie asked impatiently, awakening Michael to the reality that he was in the dressing room, still

13

holding the note from his father's old colleague. "Read it yourself," Michael said as he handed Charlie the note.

Between the two of them there were no secrets. During the *Home Revisit Program*, while traveling to historical places, Charlie had revealed to Michael that his Korean mother could have been a prostitute who abandoned him in a trash bin, and it so happened that a Catholic nun nearby heard him crying and delivered him to an orphanage.

"Wow, Michael!" Charlie said as he handed back the note, his walnut face lit with a smile, showing his white teeth. "I wish someone shows up with a note like this telling me who my father was, even if he was just a bum. I know nothing about my parents."

Michael wasn't comforted by what Charlie said. "To be honest, Charlie," he said coldly, "I don't feel exuberant about knowing that my father was a priest and that he did important things for *whoever!* If he was such a great man, why was I abandoned and sent away thousands of miles like an unwanted package? I remember the miserable day I was handed to a woman in a red dress and had to leave my mother for good. Don't tell me that a four-year-old can't remember much. I do remember many things that happened to me when I was still with her."

Charlie paid no attention to Michael. "I envy you, buddy. If I were you, I'd be dancing like this!" Leaving his clarinet case on the dressing table next to him and opening his arms wide, he twirled around, swaying his hips, saying, "*Praise the Lord, the King of Heaven! Thank you for sending me an angel to tell me who I am, thank you, thank you...*"

Michael said nothing as he stared at Charlie's silly act.

"Hey, we should celebrate, buddy," Charlie said, dropping his arms and becoming serious. "How about going for a beer? Or a glass of *Soju* (rice wine) will do. It's your choice."

"No, I'm heading home. I'm tired."

Charlie seemed offended. He picked up his clarinet case and turned to leave. "Call me anytime, Michael, if you want to talk," he said before he stepped out of the door.

Cold early winter air swept in and Michael felt a sudden chill on his back. Three other guys were in the room, he now noticed, changing into street clothes, each talking about something that happened on the stage, annoying Michael as he tried to collect his thoughts. His half-Korean, half-American face in the mirror looked back, his lips tightly sealed, forming a rigid line, while his dark-brown eyes glowed with intensity. He was lighter skinned than most Koreans and at least a head taller than most Korean males. But, his eyes were brown and his hair jet black, like other Korean males.

"Michael Hamil," he said to his reflection, "your father was a Jesuit priest who founded the first Catholic College for both men and women here in Korea. How do you feel about it?"

He cracked up. *Why should it shock me now, when I've never met him or will either?* Before this day, he had not thought much about his father, but he thought about his mother often, because he remembered her quite clearly. They lived in a Buddhist temple, in the women's quarter where men hadn't been around. Like all other nuns, his mother wore a light-gray gown made of stiff cotton under a wide-brimmed straw hat and worked in the field, like others, leaving him with an older nun who watched a dozen children, some born of the nuns, some abandoned by unwed mothers like Charlie's.

Michael's memories of his mother somewhat faded as he got older, but he still remembered her warm embrace and her smell—the smell similar to the soap his mother had used whenever she gave him a bath in a wooden tub in the kitchen. And tonight, here in the dressing room, his mother was closer to him than any time before, perhaps because the priest's note revealed unbelievable news. He tried to imagine the priest who handed Charlie the note. *Do I remember seeing a priest in the audience?* He didn't remember seeing any man in black who wore a white Roman collar.

What did Father Patrick see while he listened to our concert? Michael wondered.

The theater had been completely packed that night. The concert began with *The Promised Land in the Far East,* which Charlie had composed and sang in sextet, which sounded somewhat like African Gospel songs: '*We've come a long way, friends; and we'll walk together, thick and thin; til' we find our promised land in the Far East.*

Don't ask where the promised land is; it's there, friends, at your fingertip. Just open your eyes and see...'

15

Then, Karla Morris did her one-person play. She had golden-yellow hair and pretty, dark Asian eyes. In an ear-piercing voice, she recounted the day she lost her mother in a park at age three.

'Omma (Mother) where were you?
I looked for you for hours in the park...
I was scared when I couldn't find you! The mother of the little girl I was playing with, the lady in her Korean dress, looked for you too, and when you didn't return, she flagged a passing police car and told the police officer that you abandoned me.

'The police officer took me to the orphanage full of sick kids. They gave me a new name, Sook-hee, because I can't remember my name. I don't know how long I was there, Mother. One day, months after I got there, I was sent to America with a different name, Karla Morris. I don't know why. Omma, I wish you'd told me why you couldn't raise me and took me to an orphanage yourself. But I'm back to Seoul. The park is still there, but I can't find you where I last saw you. Omma, will I ever see you again?' The actress bent her head and wept bitterly.

The audience applauded, some wiped tears, and some shouted 'Bravo!' and whistled too.

Then it was Michael's turn. While strumming his guitar, he sang:

"My name is Orphan. My father was a zealous man who was doing great things for Koreans, my mother wrote on a note that followed me to America. This is what I figured: My father planted the seed of love in my mother but bitterly regretted it. 'Satan, leave me,' he cried and told my mother never to come see him again. My mother and I lived in a Buddhist temple, but when I turned four, she handed me to an orphanage that sent children to America, with my photo, birth certificate, and her tearful note that read, 'Son, I can't keep you, please forgive and don't look for me.'

"But I never forgot her. She was with me in that big farmhouse in Texas, in the smell of soap in the washing room,

16

and the bedroom I slept in with other boys who did farm work. Mother, you were my only home where I felt loved and safe. Someone out there, if you know where my mother lives, please tell her I'm looking for her."

He received a loud applause, as he always had. After intermission, a half-Korean, half-American woman in her early 30s gave a video presentation about 'The Korean Adoptee Revisit Program'. She talked about the history of orphan adoption services that had placed 250,000 Korean orphans, since the war ended in 1953, to some 15 different countries, mostly in the United States, and was still going strong. She showed many black and white photos of the orphans, each with a white nametag on their breasts and holding the hand of an adult, waiting to board an airplane at Kimpo Airport.

The performance ended with the announcement of the next performance and asking for donations.

How did Father Patrick find me? Michael wondered.

A loud banging on the door startled Michael. Before he responded, the door flung open and the husky Korean security guard named Song stepped in. "Why are you still here, Mr. Hamil?" he said in Korean with authority. "It's past midnight!"

"I'm sorry! I... I sort of..." Michael stammered.

"I was about to lock the building when I saw the light under the door! I could have locked you up until seven tomorrow morning!"

"I'm glad you didn't, Officer Song!" Michael jumped to his feet, quickly picked up his guitar leaning against the wall, and took his black jacket hanging on the back of his chair. Seeing the priest's note on the dressing table, he grabbed it and headed to the door.

"Good night, Mister Hamil!" Song said as Michael passed him.

"Good night, sir!"

The full moon in the cloudless sky seemed larger and brighter than he had ever seen before, and millions of stars twinkled in their mysterious languages. By contrast, the shadows of the trees on both sides of the street were dark and spooky as they swayed in the breeze. Michael walked towards the bus station, whistling the melody of '*The Promised Land in the Far East*'.

17

Chapter Two
Father Patrick

The noise of the apartment maintenance crew dragging metal trash bins on the concrete outside his window woke Michael. Remembering the letter in his coat pocket, he looked at his alarm clock on the nightstand. *7:16 AM? Would it be too early to call him*? He had no clue what time would be a good time to call a Catholic priest, yet he couldn't wait. Rising from the bed, he walked to his closet in his pajamas and dug out the note from his black coat.

He dialed the number. "Father Anderson speaking," a man's baritone voice resounded from the receiver.

For a moment, Michael didn't know what to say. His throat was too tight, and his hand holding the phone receiver trembled. "Father Anderson," he said, "I hope I'm not calling you too early. I'm Michael Hamil."

"Oh, hello, Michael! Thank you for calling!" The voice in his ear was warm and unhurried, as if he had been expecting for Michael to call.

"I received your note. Thank you so much. I want to see you as soon as you'll allow me. When would be a good time for me to come?"

"I'm about two hours away from where you performed last night, Michael. However, driving at this hour in Seoul is not wise, because of rush-hour traffic. Wait until around 9 o'clock, then you can get here in Sochun in two hours. And plan to have lunch with me here, at my place, so we have plenty of time to visit."

"That's very kind of you, Father," Michael said, somewhat relaxed. "I can't wait to see you, Father!"

"Same here," the priest said. He then gave him the driving instructions and Michael jotted them down.

"I'll be looking out for you around 11 o'clock," Father Patrick said. "And drive carefully!"

"I will, Father. See you soon."

After the phone clicked off, Michael didn't move, still holding the phone receiver against his ear, as if he thought the old priest might say more. It seemed unreal that he'd soon meet him, a priest who had known his father since his seminary days and worked with him later too, at the college his father had founded, here in Seoul.

At 9 AM, Michael drove his Hyundai Sonata out of the parking spot in front of his apartment on the first floor and headed south, remembering Father Anderson's warning 'Drive carefully'.

What would he ask me? he thought. *And where should I begin when he asks about my childhood? He would not know anything about me. How would he, unless he had known my mother? I will tell him about the farmhouse I lived in and the older boys who taught me many things in life—scavenging, lying, begging, and stealing, but also good things, like how to catch lizards, frogs, and snakes with bare hands.*

In the farmhouse, beside himself and the owners, Papa and Mama Hamil, lived four older boys—Tom, Aaron, Max, and Scott—not counting three huge dogs. The older boys spent all day with Papa Hamil in the farm, changing straw in the goat den or in the chicken coop or fetching water from the deep well and delivering it, in wooden buckets, for humans as well as for animals—cows, goats, rabbits, and chickens. Papa and Mama Hamil didn't send any of the boys to school, but then Michael didn't know what school was all about or that every kid older than five years had to attend school every day, five days a week, except during the school breaks.

When Michael was old enough, he too worked along with the older boys—changing hay in the barns or collecting eggs from the chicken coop—but he didn't carry the water buckets because they were too heavy for him.

When he was 11, he ran away from Papa's farm with Max, the boy 2 years older than Michael himself, who had tattoos on his arms. They had fun, sleeping in a big abandoned house in

19

the woods that had been boarded up for some years. Max had evidently stolen money from selling eggs without the owners knowing about it and bought hotdogs from the food vendors and shared them with Michael. Sometimes, they stole fruit or crackers from the vendors and ate them by the pond next to the vacant home and fed the ducks with the leftovers. And this was when Michael learned to smoke cigarettes that Max gave him to 'try'.

We could have lived there forever, had the police not shown up, Michael thought to himself... *But I won't tell Father Patrick about how Max and I ended up in jail.*

Besides stealing food from the vendors after Max's stolen money had run out, Max and he went door-to-door, offering to mow the lawns or to do any kind of work for money. Some people handed them a dollar or two or apples or bananas, but most of them didn't even open the door for them.

Two men named Jimmy and Bob, who lived in a small house on the other side of the main street from the vacant home the boys lived in, were different; they offered the boys work and invited them in and even fed them occasionally. Jimmy was taller than Bob and pale-skinned, but Bob was sun-tanned and had bulging muscles. They were both in their early 30s and were self-proclaimed Street Artists who sold their paintings on the street or drew instant portraits of people who paid them. Michael and Max cleaned their junk-filled two-bedroom home, garage, and basement and washed their old red Mustang inside and out. On weekends, the boys helped them move their painted canvases to the street in the morning and brought them back to their house at dusk.

One evening, Bob and Jimmy complimented them for the job well done and invited them to dinner—a dinner of barbecued pork ribs and corn on the cob. Afterwards, Bob asked them if they'd deliver a small package to their 'friend' named 'Phil' a mile away for ten dollars each.

Michael and Max were elated. Ten dollars could buy ten packages of hotdogs, or ten juicy double cheeseburgers, or a bag of groceries. The instructions were simple enough. "When my friend Phil opens the door, just give this parcel and leave. If Phil asks you questions, tell him to call me. We'll be watching you."

"No problem!" they chorused.

But things didn't go the way they had expected. In fact, it was a nightmare. After Bob and Jimmy dropped them off in front of an old house with torn awnings and peeling paint, they walked to the door together. Max rang the doorbell. A middle-aged man wearing a gray shirt over a pair of jeans peeked out. "What do you want?" he asked in an unfriendly voice.

Max thrust the package, saying, "This is from Jimmy and Bob. Bob said you should call him if you have a question."

Instead of Phil taking the box, he vanished behind the door and the door flung open and a policeman rushed out. "Don't move, boys," the policeman hissed breathlessly. Max dropped the box and screamed at the same time. The policeman then forced Max to turn around and handcuffed him, while Max protested, saying that he was only doing this job for two men who had hired him. "Isn't this house owned by a guy named Phil?" he asked.

"Yes, it is!"

"Then why are you doing this to me?"

"You'll soon find out what you did wrong, okay?"

Michael didn't wait to find out. Quickly, he turned around and ran to where Bob and Jimmy had dropped them off and driven away, though they weren't there anymore. The policeman followed him. Michael changed directions and ran towards the next block, in vague hopes that Bob and Jimmy would show up and rescue him. The next thing he knew, the officer had knocked him onto the ground. Dirt jumped onto his face and he struggled to breathe. The policeman forced his arms to his back and handcuffed him, hurting him.

The policeman took Max and Michael to a juvenile detention center that night. Two days later, in a courtroom, they learned that what they had attempted to deliver to Phil was an illegal drug called heroin. During the interrogations, they had spelled out Bob and Jimmy's names and where they lived, but that didn't give them freedom; a few vendors they had stolen hotdogs and cigarettes from showed up and testified that the boys were thieves. They were locked up behind bars with other 'troublemakers' for months, not knowing when they could get out. One day, Max got into a fight with rough-looking, dark-skinned boys who couldn't speak a word of English and a

21

prison guard came and took Max and the rough boys somewhere. Michael never saw him again.

* * *

Around 11 o'clock, Michael saw a wooden sign that read 'Sochun Catholic Church' on the side of the road and veered his Hyundai Sonata into the dirt road where the arrow sign pointed. On his right stood a long white picket fence keeping a few sheep, pigs, and chickens from wandering about, and on the left lay a cornfield full of colorless, dried cornstalks. Straight ahead was a church with a steeple with a bell tower.

As he approached the church, he saw a tall American priest standing on the front steps, his hands behind him, and as soon as he saw the car, he waved.

Michael honked his car horn, glad that he had come to the right church. He parked next to the church, on a concrete patch marked with white lines, and got out.

Father Anderson rushed to him. "Thank you for coming," he said in fluent Korean, his eyes glowing with excitement.

"It's my pleasure, Father," Michael said in Korean as well.

They shook hands.

"Did you find the church okay?"

"Yes, Father. Your instructions were perfect."

"I forgot to tell you about the road construction on the highway, but it must not have been a problem for you."

"I didn't see any signs of construction, Father. Maybe it was complete just in time for me."

The priest laughed. "Probably you're right. You must have inherited a sense of humor from your father."

"I must have. I feel I know him now."

They entered the church, lit by sunlight entering through stained glass windows facing south. As they passed the front of the church in the raised area with the alter table and tabernacle, Father Anderson knelt on the marble step and lowered his head.

Michael stood awkwardly next to the pew and waited for him. He had been in a church only a few times as an adult, mostly for weddings of his friends; and he had no urge to kneel next to the priest, whom he had just met, and pretend to be praying to the god who had called his father to priesthood and

22

brought him to Korea to do *important* work for the Korean people. To him, God was a stranger.

Father Patrick didn't pray long. Making a sign of the cross, he raised himself slowly to a standing position. Michael then realized that the old man might be suffering arthritis in his legs, which he had not noticed outside.

"Please, follow me," Father Patrick said and walked ahead. They turned two corners in the narrow corridor, where many framed pictures of ancient churches hung, and entered a room.

"Come in, come in," Father Patrick said. The room smelled of old pine, and against each wall stood a tall bookcase. One of the bookcases held a framed black and white photo in which several American priests were posing with two Korean priests. Michael was sad that he couldn't identify his father, if he was among them.

He wasn't eager to ask Father Patrick if his father was in the photo. What did it matter after all these years? He was a stranger to him, as John F. Kennedy was.

Michael sat on a grey sofa, as Father Patrick had motioned him to sit, and waited for the old priest to seat himself on the matching chair opposite him. Here, seated only three feet from him, Michael noticed that Father Patrick indeed resembled the famous American author Ernest Hemingway, with white hair and a gentle expression on his wrinkled face.

He had read Hemingway's book *An Old Man and the Sea* and loved it. The book gave him an urge to go to the ocean and be on a dingy and fish all day. But that had not happened yet.

"You have some of your father's Irish facial features," Father Anderson said, his gaze lingering on him.

"You think so, Father?" Michael asked.

"Yes, you are his son!"

Michael chuckled. "When I was a kid growing up in Austin, many people thought I was a Chinese boy because of my dark-brown eyes and black hair. But here, kids call me, 'American Uncle'!"

Father Patrick smiled. "Your father would be proud of you, Michael, if he were here…"

Michael felt a sting in his eyes. "I don't know about that, Father."

23

"Why do you say that? You're a handsome young man who's an accomplished musician."

Michael shifted his gaze to a bookcase on the wall and stared. "Isn't it obvious, Father? He didn't want to acknowledge my existence, his son, conceived with a Korean woman. If he had the courage to admit his involvement with my mother and acknowledged me, he wouldn't have done what he did to my mother and me."

Father Patrick didn't respond for a brief moment, his facial muscles tightening, but when he spoke, he exuded certain authority. "You must understand his situation at the time, Michael. It's not as simple as you think. His responsibility as the founder and dean of the first American Catholic College in South Korea was enormous. He represented the American Jesuits to Koreans, to say the least. Had he acknowledged his involvement with your mother, a student at the time, and your impending birth, he would've had no choice but to step down from his position. Had he done that, it'd have been such a blow to the Jesuit Fathers working with him at the school, not to mention the Fathers in Milwaukee, in the Wisconsin Province, where your father was ordained and trained as a missionary."

Michael turned to look at Father Patrick. "So in your opinion, he did the right thing!"

"Yes. I believe your father might have considered stepping down and leaving the school, but he couldn't actually do it, because no other Jesuits spoke Korean as well as your father, nor was anyone else as knowledgeable about Korean history, its people, and where the country stood at the time as he was."

"Oh, I get it, Father," Michael said in a sarcastic tone of voice. "What God wanted him to do for Koreans was far more important for him than the *life* he caused to happen, isn't that so? But what about the young woman's life he ruined?"

"Wait, you can't make that quick judgment…"

Michael ignored him. "And my mother was a Korean woman. That explains everything, doesn't it? Why would an American priest leave his vocation and what he had accomplished here and marry a young Korean girl and stain his pristine reputation? I can't help but wonder whether he would've done the same, had the woman been an American white woman working for a prestigious American company."

"That has nothing to do with why your father chose what he did," Father Patrick said in a subdued voice.

"I believe it did. He was all wrapped up in the importance of his work and his own reputation and severed his relationship with my mother, giving her no choice but to send me away to America to never see me again." His voice cracking, Michael bent his head and remained in that posture.

Father Patrick's wrinkles between his eyes deepened as he said, "Your father deserves understanding for the choice he made for the school's sake. And he's no longer in this world, Michael. He was human, like you and I are. We all have weaknesses."

Michael lifted his tear-stricken face and spoke slowly, "Yes, he had weaknesses, for sure. Do you know what it's like not knowing where you came from? People seem to think that an orphan is a child with no parents. But an orphan grows up, becomes an adult, and inside he's still an orphan, without anyone to trust, without anyone claiming him as their son or daughter. Even today, I feel I have no identity, Father, like a rock buried in dirt! My name Michael Hamil isn't the name my natural parents gave me at birth, but the couple in Texas who adopted me for a selfish reason—a future farm hand. I grew up with four older boys, sharing the bed with them, and gruel that had no taste. Is it surprising to you that I'm bitter about my fate?"

"I hear you!" Father Patrick said in a business-like tone. "But there are better things to focus on in this world than being bitter about your fate all your life, Michael. Don't underestimate Satan's power to turn people against God using their anger."

"Satan, Father?" Michael said, losing vitality in his voice.

"Yes. Satan lurks out unexpectedly from men's cores to create hell on earth. Without talking about Judas and Peter, Jesus' apostles who betrayed their Master, Satan lives with us, here on earth. Think about the North Korean leaders. They are creating hell for their people. Satan is as real as God Himself is."

Michael quietly stared the floor before him without a word.

"Don't you want to know how I found you?" Father Patrick asked, changing the subject.

"I was about to ask you that, Father. How did you hear about me, that I was singing with the band or that I'm my father's son? After I read your note last night, I couldn't sleep."

"A friend of mine, Sister Angela, who's also from Milwaukee and has worked with your father as a young nun, told me about you. Among a few of us missionaries, his scandal with a student was no secret. Sister Angela told me that she read about your band, 'The Returned', performing at that theater some time ago, and out of curiosity, she and her friend attended it. The moment she saw you, she knew you could be Father Dolan's son. She urged me to go see for myself. It's a small world, isn't it?"

"Did Sister Angela know my mother?"

"I don't think so."

"How about you, Father? Did you know my mother when she was a student at the College?"

"Yes. Your mother, Min-sook Hyon, was in my class in 1972, my last year with Sonam College. I mostly remember her as an outstanding pianist, besides being a serious student who eagerly participated in class. Whenever the College invited the board members and city officials for fundraising purposes, your mother entertained the guests. I remember her performance of Chopin's Polonaise and Beethoven's Moonlight Sonata quite vividly still. She..." he paused briefly, searching for words. "She definitely played with a lot of feelings and virtuosity."

"Wow! I can't believe that my mother was in your class. Were you aware that she was expecting me?"

"No, I was not. I didn't know anything about it until an unexpected faculty meeting was held in your father's office one late afternoon. The topic shocked me: *Should we allow two pregnant female students to continue to attend the College?* It was your father who had called an urgent faculty meeting that night and all 30 members attended. I can't recall how he began the meeting, but we had a long discussion about it, talking about the College's reputation and how Korean society would judge it had we allowed them to attend. Most of the American professors and staff members among us, including myself, were against expelling the two students for being pregnant. But the only Korean priest among us, Father Moon, was staunchly against letting them continue their study. He kept saying that this was Korea, not America, and that Koreans don't think like Americans. 'And this is a Catholic college!' he said over and over. 'Women with bulging bellies don't belong here! They'll make our College look bad. Did you know an ancient Korean Proverb that says, 'A sea worm can ruin a fish market's reputation?"

"Wait, Father," Michael interrupted. "Am I hearing right, that my father suggested to remove my mother and another pregnant student from the College?"

"Yes. But at the meeting, he didn't mention the names of the pregnant students. Only later, when the decision was made to suspend them from school until they gave birth, did we all hear the names. But no one suspected anything about his involvement with your mother."

"My question is: wasn't he aware that he himself caused my mother to conceive me?" Michael sounded angry.

"Some of us who had been aware of his secret meetings with your mother asked that question after your mother and the other student were expelled temporarily. Of course, none of them returned. But looking back now, I understand why he had to put Min-sook out of his sight so that he could go on with his work. Do you understand?"

Michael shook his head. "No, I don't. But tell me, Father, why did you leave Korea? You wrote in your note that 1972 was your last year with Sonam College. Does it have anything to do with my father?"

"Yes and no. It was the year the South Korean president Park Jung-hee made two grave mistakes: he drastically increased the number of South Korean troops fighting in Vietnam along with the Americans, and he also extended his presidential term until his death, ignoring the law that prevented any president serving for more than two four-year terms, same as in the U.S. When people rallied against the new laws, asking the president to step down, he ordered the military to crack down on the demonstrators. Your father was seriously against Sonam students rallying against the government's policies. All student meetings in the campus were banned and anyone attempting to hold such meetings would be punished without exceptions. And he actually expelled a few students caught by the police while they mingled with demonstrators.

That made the situation far worse, Michael. The whole body of students exploded with anger one day. They walked out of classrooms while their instructors were talking!

"And that happened during my class. One morning, I followed my students to the Shinchon Rotary, unable to stop them from joining the demonstrators. Should I go on?"

"Yes, please. I know nothing about what happened here in Korea. Were you arrested for being with demonstrators?"

"I was. My crime was for protecting my students by pleading with policemen to please stop hurting them. They beat me with their clubs, like they did the students, even though I was in my black and had the Roman collar. That's how brutal the policemen were. I fought back by throwing my fists into their faces. Remember, I'm at least a foot taller than them."

"Wow! I wish I was there to see that!"

"No, you don't! You'd have been beaten too."

"Did my father fire you for that? Is that why you left Korea?"

"He had to fire me, Michael, after he saw my picture on the front page of the newspaper, under the caption, '*American priest raged*'. The photographer, whoever he was, did a fine job to show international readers how brutally the policemen were beating, not only their own kind, but also an American priest. My actions against police brutality towards unarmed civilians made a huge impact in Korea as well as in the U.S., including the Jesuit Fathers in Wisconsin province."

"Was leaving the country your choice?

"No, I was ordered to by a Korean court for disobeying the security law and my superior in Milwaukee sent me a plane ticket in a hurry. When you're a priest, you can't beat anyone, even those who beat you."

The phone on his desk rang loudly, and Father Patrick rose and reached for the phone on his desk. "Father Patrick Anderson speaking," he said. After a few 'yes's and solemn nodding, he said, "I'll be there as soon as I can," and hung up. Turning to Michael, he said, "I'm very sorry to end our meeting like this, Michael, but a chaplain at Saint Joseph Hospital informed me that the parishioner I've been visiting since spring has just died and that I must come immediately."

"I'm sorry too, Father. When can I come see you again?"

"How about this Saturday afternoon?"

"That'd be great."

"I want you to meet with Father James Murphy, your father's successor at Sonam College. He retired a couple years ago as the dean but is still teaching History of Western Religion as professor emeritus."

"Father, does Father Murphy know I exist?"

"I've told him about you, yes."

Michael grimaced. "Father… I'm not comfortable about meeting him. I don't know what to tell him. I can't say, '*I'm Father John Dolan's son. Good meeting with you, Father Murphy'*."

"Michael, I have a good reason for encouraging you to meet with him. Ten years ago, when I returned to Korea for the second time, he called me and asked if I wanted to come and pick up a box of your father's belongings still in his attic—his Omega watch, ring, diary, letters, and newspaper articles about him in Seoul. At that time, I didn't want to look at them because I had difficulties in dealing with my old memories of him. But it's different now. You're the rightful owner of your father's lifetime belongings."

"Can I think about it, Father?" he asked, without looking at the priest. "Things are happening too quickly for me."

"I have a better idea. Call me if you decided not to go with me, because Father Murphy is getting old and he wants to dispose of your father's things before something happens to him. I'll see you at school at two. It's easy to find once you take Shinchon exit from the highway."

Chapter Three
Doctor Kim, a Vietnam War Veteran

That night, returning from performing the final rites on a widower who had been battling his lung cancer for months at St. Joseph Hospital, Father Patrick found himself in a gloomy mood. First, he had to leave Michael to hurry to the hospital without offering him lunch, which he had promised him. And secondly, after anointing the dead he had noticed nagging feelings about his own death, which would certainly come, whether he liked it or not. He had no health problem to worry about, but lately he had been lethargic and the arthritis in his left leg seemed to be getting worse. Who was exempted from dying? He had passed his 68th birthday a month earlier. With that in mind, he wanted to see his former student Dr Kim Youn-Gill, who had fought in the Vietnam War as a result of President Park's troop deployment policy and was now a well-distinguished surgeon who also taught at Seoul National University's School of Medicine. Dr. Kim could certainly help Michael in some way, if something happened to himself. Who else can help? And Kim saw Father Dolan's corpse as an intern at Seoul University Medical Center's forensic lab. *I'll give him a call.*

The phone kept ringing, and when he was about to give up, Dr. Kim's voice rang in his ear, "Hello?"

"Dr. Kim, I'm glad I caught you."

"I'm glad you did too, Father. What's up?"

"I'm coming to Seoul tomorrow afternoon and I'm wondering if we could have lunch at the same restaurant we've met at a few times."

"That'd be great, Father. It's been awhile since I last saw you. Is everything alright?"

"Of course!"

30

"Great! I'll wait for you at Red Dragon at noon."

The next day at noon, Red Dragon was busy. Dr. Kim seated himself at a table by the window, and a young waitress wearing a bright-pink dress rushed over and served him steamy tea. The colorful wall decorations showing a fire-breathing dragon were still the same, but the owner was different. There used to be a toothless grandpa who would greet him with a smile, but now a young woman in her 30s did without a smile. The first time he had met Father Patrick here, in this restaurant, was 10 years ago, in the fall of 1992, shortly after Father Patrick returned to Korea for the second time, having lived in Milwaukee for 20 years. It was a great reunion for both; the reunion that re-bonded them together.

Father Patrick had been well-loved by all the students, particularly when Korean troops were sent to Vietnam by the thousands each day and their future seemed bleak. Every student he knew worried that they would not come back to finish college. It was an uncertain time for sure, particularly when the American dean did nothing to stop the government from sending Korean troops to Vietnam. Rather, it seemed that the dean supported government policy, by banning the students from gathering for meetings and posting threats all over the campus.

But Father Patrick understood how the Korean 'boys' felt about leaving for Vietnam and fighting for people they didn't know or cared for at the possibility of their own death. Kim still remembered the morning the whole class marched out of Father Patrick's philosophy class, in spite of his urging not to demonstrate and get caught by armed policemen. It was the morning the president had re-emphasized his non-negotiable power as well as his unlimited time to rule, through the radio, adding that anyone violating the laws of national security would be severely punished.

But once they walked out of the classroom, no one listened to Father Patrick, which had never happened before; and he followed them to Shinchon Square, where a large crowd had gathered. Shouts from men and women were louder than a train passing by as two dozen policemen wearing tear gas masks wielded their clubs with dexterity.

The students ignored the yellow barricades blocking them and invited themselves into the center of the crowd. Police clubs landed on them, making percussion music. The more they were beaten, the harder the students fought. A few men and women fell, their faces bloody. Father Patrick pulled the arm of a policeman who was beating one of the students, asking him please stop hurting him. But, the policeman instead grabbed Father Patrick's arms and forced him to turn around and walk away from his students. Father Patrick fought not to leave. Everyone heard his frantic voice, saying, "You can't do this to my students. I'm their teacher!"

The policeman barked, "Don't stick your long nose into our business, Yankee Preacher. Get lost, now!" As Father Patrick bolted from the policeman and turned around to free himself, another policeman came and hit him on the head with his club. Father Patrick seemed to falter, but he turned around and threw his fists into the face of his assailant. Two policemen grabbed him from each side and took him to a police car parked on the curb. The car door opened and he was thrown into the back seat and the car drove away, its siren loud and ear-piercing. Soon afterwards, he left Korea. Rumors had said that he was deported to the U.S. for beating law-enforcement officers. Some others believed that the dean had sent him back to the Jesuit Father's community in Milwaukee.

Ten years earlier, in this restaurant, Kim saw Father Patrick in tears while looking through photos of his old students who fought in Vietnam in the album Kim had brought with him. They were awful photos, showing piles of corpses lying on the roadside, or burning shacks with straw-thatched roofs, or dead soldiers hanging from trees in a jungle. Kim was glad that he had not told Father Patrick about Yang Chil-suk, his classmate who had regularly served Father Patrick as an altar boy during Sunday Mass. Yang had died while he and two others landed from a helicopter to pick up injured soldiers, when they accidentally stepped on a live powerline buried under dried palm leaves and broken bricks. Father Patrick's grief would have been worse had he told him about Yang's tragic end amidst war debris in a faraway land.

Father Patrick walked in. Youn-gill waved, saying, "Here, Father Patrick!" Seeing him, Father Patrick waved too and rushed over. "Dr. Kim! How glad I am to see you!"

Youn-gill sprang to his feet and saluted him in military fashion. They shook hands.

"It's so good to see you, Father Patrick!"

"You look distinguished with gray hair."

"Thank you, Father. Believe it or not, I'm the oldest in my surgical team."

"I say *life* begins at 60. You have a few more years to get there yet."

Youn-gill laughed. "Is it from your experience, Father, that life begins at 60?"

"Yes, trust me!"

The same waitress in pink came with a notepad and Youn-gill ordered Seafood Casserole, a spicy dish they both liked.

Father Patrick seemed anxious to talk. "Dr. Kim, I remember you telling me that you identified Father Dolan's body while you were an intern at the Seoul University Medical School forensic lab."

"Yes, Father."

"I have some news for you." He quickly looked around, as if he were about to reveal a secret. "As unbelievable as it seems, I met Father Dolan's son yesterday."

"What?"

"It's true. He's a singer belonging to a band called *The Returned*." He told Kim how he found out about the band made of all half-American, half-Korean men that performed every Friday night at a theater in Itaewon, and that he had heard them two days earlier.

"The young man's name is Michael Hamil; Hamil being his adoptive father's name in Texas. He asked me many questions about his father and I told him as much as I could. And I thought he might want to find out how his father had died, at some point. That's why I thought about you, Dr. Kim. You're the only one who saw his father's body."

Youn-gill's expression turned rigid. "How can you be sure about it, Father, that this guy is Father Dolan's son?"

"He looks much like Father Dolan, Dr. Kim, for one thing. He's tall and has that Irish face with dark eyes and dark, curly hair, but one might notice his yellowish Asian skin and facial features. Another thing is that he said his mother wrote a note about his father being a very important man doing important things for Koreans and sent it with him to his adoptive parents' home in Texas. After meeting him in person, I'm pretty convinced that he's our former dean's son."

Kim made a long, cold expression before he blurted, "Women can lie many *white* lies."

"What do you mean by that?"

Kim smacked his lips gravely and then said, "I've never told you this, but I supposedly fathered a child while I was in Vietnam, some 30 years ago."

"What…?"

"Yes! It's a long story, Father. I don't know how to tell you…"

"You don't have to tell me anything, Dr. Kim, if you don't want to."

"It's not that I don't want to talk about it, Father, but I'm afraid that you wouldn't want to believe it. There were a couple of bar girls I spent time with when we were off-duty. Right after the news that Saigon fell to the North Vietnamese Army and that we'd soon evacuate reached us, my commander, Lieutenant Shin, sent for me. This guy was a heartless bastard, Father, who enjoyed punishing guys. In his tent, he looked angry as I saluted him. 'Is it true?' he barked at me. 'I don't know what you're talking about, sir,' I said. 'Private Kim. Don't play games with me, okay?' he said. Knowing his temper, I just stood there, awaiting an explanation. He said that a village girl had come to see him earlier that day, saying that she was carrying my child!"

"Was that true?" Father Patrick asked.

"I don't know, Father. The truth is I had been so drunk some nights at the bar that I couldn't even remember who I was with or what I did. *'What's the girl's name? What did she look like?'* I asked the lieutenant. And he blew his top off, saying, 'It doesn't matter who you were with or what you did. The bottom line is, we Korean soldiers came here as their liberators! We don't want to leave our dirty paw prints here, in Vietnam, understand? There have been complaints against us by the villagers—some saying that our soldiers killed their buffalos or

34

raped their wives or daughters. Some say our jeep ran over their children, injuring them badly.' When I blankly stared at the lieutenant, he dismissed me with a simple wave of his hand. Later, I received a letter from the ROK saying that the army would settle my case with the native people and that I would hear from them again. I felt like a bargain chip on a game table."

"Have you confirmed the truth of the woman's claim?"

"I could not, Father, because we were banned from going into the village that very same day I heard the news and a month later, we evacuated. That's the reason I'm not ready to believe what you've just told me; that Father Dolan had an illegitimate son. It's probably a fabricated story."

"How did the ROK Army handle your case?"

"The army reduced my salary and pension drastically to pay my accuser. I was afraid that the woman would show up in Seoul, to find me and claim that I was the father of her kid, but it never happened. Losing a chunk of money from my salary and benefit wasn't a big deal for me, because the hospital paid me well after I graduated as a certified surgeon. But the experience—the false accusation and humiliation—made me a bitter man. That's why I never married, Father. The whole thing still haunts me."

Father Patrick nodded sympathetically. "I'm sorry to hear that, Dr. Kim. Today, many men prefer living alone, not just Catholic clergy."

"Father, I don't want to shock you, but I'm gay! I was raised in a Catholic church and attended Sonam Catholic College for three years, but God left me shortly after we arrived in Vietnam. I have no regrets about my decisions."

"Do you think I'm judgmental about your lifestyle?"

"But the Church is!"

Father let out a long sigh. "The Church isn't perfect. The Church will change."

Food arrived. But Kim couldn't enjoy food.

Father Patrick began eating. Or was he pretending to eat?

Chapter Four
The Graveyard Keeper

After lunch, Father Patrick and Dr. Kim parted with handshakes. Dr. Kim watched Father Patrick as he walked to his old gray Toyota parked under a maple tree in front of the restaurant, get in, and drive out, perhaps heading for a monthly missionary meeting somewhere.

Kim felt as though he had offended Father Patrick by revealing that he was gay, which he had not told anyone like he had today. But what was done was done.

He had barely touched the food after he had talked about the Vietnamese bar girl who had given him nightmares and made him distrustful of women, except his mother, who had passed away at the age 82 a year ago. *And why did Father Patrick think I could help the young man who's supposedly Father Dolan's son?*

Dean Dolan did nothing for us students, he bitterly remembered. *He agreed with our president, Park Chung-hee— a former army lieutenant general who had succeeded in a military coup and became the president by public vote in early 1960s—about sending Korean troops to Vietnam. It was no secret that Park's primary purpose was to gain American dollars so that Park could modernize his country, which had been badly damaged during a three-year war a decade earlier.*

As a result of offering Korean troops to the Vietnam War like sacrificial animals, the American President Johnson supplied the Park administration weapons, tanks, other war-machines, and battle gear for each of the more than 300,000 Korean soldiers during 10 years, between 1963 and 1973. Of those who fought in Vietnam, more than 5,000 Koreans were killed and 11,000 wounded. And that didn't count those who died at home from exposure to Agent Orange years later, the powerful chemical American air fighters sprayed to eliminate enemy hiding in the jungles, as well as to destroy forest cover and crops for the North Vietnamese Army and Viet Cong troops.

The Park administration received hundreds of millions of American dollars for sending troops, and most of the funds were spent to rebuild the country from the previous war's devastation. The money funded construction of new highways, high-rise commercial buildings, apartment buildings, and the government's expenses.

Dr. Kim had not been surprised when President Park was assassinated in 1979. He was killed by his *coup d'etat* buddy for the wrong reason, yet Kim felt that justice was served by the power above human power.

Kim didn't have a particular goal for the afternoon because he had taken the day off for lunch with Father Patrick. He thought about visiting White Horse café owned and operated by one of his Vietnam War veteran friends, nicknamed 'Shorty'. Shorty lost his left eye to a grenade that exploded in the bunker where his unit was hiding and spent a month in the hospital. As a one-eyed man, Shorty had a remarkable attitude about life: he wasn't bitter about what he had lost and was successful in the liquor business. But as he approached the bar, Kim thought it was too early to be in the Café, because none of his veteran friends would be there.

He decided to visit Kang Jung-soo instead, one of the twins who had served in the same ROK Army company in a village near Quinon where Kim himself had been a platoon leader. Jung-soo survived the war, but his twin, Jung-hoon, did not. Jung-hoon was one of the last Korean soldiers killed after news came that the war had ended with Saigon falling into enemy hands.

It was during a morning assembly when the commander broke the news that their night patrol team had been attacked and all four men, including Private Kang Jung-hoon, had been killed.

Jung-soo was beyond himself. He wanted to find his brother's killer and serve him justice in the spirit of 'eye for eye; tooth for tooth'. But the company commander wouldn't let him go. Two weeks later, the company began to evacuate the area, but Jung-soo refused to cooperate, crying and saying, "How can I go home without my brother? What'll my mother say? She's waiting for both of us."

The commander yelled at him: "Your widowed mother will die of heartbreak when *no son* of hers returns alive. How can you do such a thing to your single mom? And if you stay here, you wouldn't survive a single day. Remember, North Vietnam took over the country! You'll be captured or killed before the day is over!"

After returning from Vietnam, Jung-soo applied for a job at the National Cemetery as a grave-keeper while others returned to school or applied for well-paying jobs with the support of the government. And ever since, Jung-soo devoutly maintained the cemetery lot in a meticulous condition and seemed to be satisfied.

It took Kim almost an hour to reach the exit sign that read 'Seoul National Cemetery'. The Vietnam War Veterans Memorial sat on a hillside. Kim parked his Kia behind a wooden building shaded by tall pines with the sign 'Veterans Only' and walked towards the sea of white crosses ahead of him. He remembered reading U.S. WWII Admiral Nimitz's famous quote posted in the Washington Memorial Park: *'They fought together as brothers in arms; they died together and now they sleep side-by-side. To them we have a solemn obligation—the obligation to ensure that their sacrifices will help make this a better and safer world.'*

The whole place was silently dormant this morning, except for the sounds of cars on a distant highway he couldn't see. Some men laying here had been in the same company Kim himself had been on that cursed ground, in the sweltering heat for two years. Some were barely 18, even younger than he had been at that time. Where were they now? Heaven? Hell? Purgatory? Everyone buried here had once belonged to someone and gone to school, like Kim himself had. But now, the only ID they shared among them were the white wooden crosses, each with a name, birth and death date, and a military rank that meant nothing anymore.

Kim had an urge to tear down the invisible wall that stood between himself and these silent occupants and shout 'Wake

38

up, guys! You've been sleeping too long!' But he only stood there, feeling a lump rising in his throat.

Kim heard noises of feet moving behind him. Turning, he saw a short man wearing loosely fitting work clothes and a familiar baseball cap with the logo of the Vietnam War Veterans embroidered in gold threads. "Kang Jung-soo!" Kim called out.

Kang stopped walking, his head turning this way and that. Upon seeing him, he shouted, "Sergeant Kim!" and ran toward him. "What are you doing here?"

They embraced.

"How busy are you, Jung-soo?" Kim asked, straightening himself.

"I'm not busy at all, Sergeant Kim. What's on your mind?"

"Stop calling me Sergeant Kim," he said. "The war ended almost 30 years ago, buddy."

Jung-soo laughed. "You're still my boss, Sergeant! I won't call you any other way even if you want to shoot me."

"Okay, do it your way!" Kim said. "Can we talk?"

"Of course. Let's go to the shrine up on the hill. It's nice and warm on a sunny day like this. And there are benches where we can sit." They walked side-by-side along the hedges that divided the burial plots from the parking area.

"Do you still like working here?" Kim asked casually.

"I do. It's peaceful and there's plenty of things for me to do. And I'm close to my brother and all my combat buddies from Vietnam."

"Don't you get lonely here? Don't you miss going to a bar and having a good time with… you know?"

"No. My brother doesn't like it. And I don't miss anything from what we used to do in Vietnam. The whole country was pure hell."

"Tell me about it," Kim said. "It was a godless place for sure."

"I know what you mean, Sergeant. The jungle where we fought was a slaughterhouse where you're supposed to kill or die. Nothing in between! Out of fear, I always prayed for our safety, but the Vietcong always found us and chased us shooting! How many times did we all return to our camp safely? We always lost a few guys, if not a dozen! I hated it.

39

Even after I came back home, I had a strange feeling about going to the church I used to belong to. As soon as I knelt at the pew, God seemed to say, 'You killed my people in Vietnam. Didn't I say, *Thou shalt not kill?*' So I ended up not going to church anymore."

"The Bible says God loves everyone, even your sworn enemy," Kim said. "I was never comforted by simply praying. Looking back, praying is stupid when your enemy is chasing to kill. While praying, you close your eyes and relax, forgetting where you are or what you're doing, allowing your enemy a perfect chance to attack you. Many guys prayed while bullets whizzed by and ended up dying. At boot camp, we should have learned not to pray while fighting. But no one taught us that!"

"Makes sense, Sergeant," Kang said. "I sometimes wonder whether my brother was praying the night he was killed. It's possible. He was more religious than I was. How can you watch snipers while praying, eyes closed? If he had been alert, he might be alive today."

The shrine was wide open to the sky, with a view of distant mountains. The sunlight was warm and the red granite walls bearing 5001 names, names of the fallen soldiers, reflected the sunlight. The dazzling white marble statue of four soldiers lifting a large flagpole with a Korean flag towards the blue sky overhead seemed most appropriate for a place like this. They sat on one of the wooden benches facing the statue.

"Sergeant, do you have a cigarette?" Jung-soo asked.

Kim produced a pack from his shirt pocket and handed one to Jung-soo and took one for himself.

"What made you find me here today, Sergeant?" Jung-soo asked.

"I have something to tell you."

"I'm listening, Sergeant," he said, blowing smoke towards the blue above.

Kim briefed him about what Father Patrick had said—that Dean Dolan had a son, who grew up in the U.S. but returned to Seoul and now lived in Shinchon, singing with a band. "Father Patrick said that he met the guy two days ago and found him so much like Father Dolan, except his Asian skin and whatever."

"Wow, what a story!" Jung-soo said.

"Surprisingly enough, Father Patrick thought I should meet the guy, since I saw his father's corpse at the forensic lab where I was an intern after returning from Vietnam. Remember, he was found in a creek, all bruised-up and a bullet hole in the back of his head? Father Patrick said that this guy, Michael Hamil, deserves to know about his father, including how his father died. Does it make sense, Jung-soo? It's been nearly 30 years since I saw him in the forensic lab. I'm sure you read about his death in the papers."

"Sure, I did. And you told us about it at one of our meetings. It was big news then. What did you tell Father Patrick?"

"I didn't want to say yes and I couldn't say no, so I told him I'd think about it. But the more I think about it, the more I don't like the idea. What's the purpose of meeting the son of the dean who didn't raise a finger for us when our government was sending us to Vietnam to fight?"

"Knowing Father Patrick, I'm not surprised. He thinks highly of you, Sergeant. He'd not have asked if he didn't trust you. What harm would there be in meeting the guy: what was his name, again?

"*Michael Hamil*. Hamil is the family name of the couple in Texas who adopted him."

"If I were Dean Dolan's son," said Kang, blowing another stream of smoke into the air, "I'd definitely want to meet the doctor who examined my father's corpse, even though it'd give me nightmares for days or for months. A son has the right to know how his father died, I think. And in this case, he could have been murdered."

"The case is still open as an 'unsolved murder'. Remember the janitor named Wong who defected from the North? He was arrested as one of the suspects but was released almost immediately."

"I sure do. Didn't he disappear mysteriously?"

"That's the problem. If the media hears about this guy, who's supposedly Father Dolan's son, the detectives will snoop around us Vietnam veterans like they did 30 years ago. A bunch of us were interrogated at the time but no one was arrested."

"The policeman came to talk to me twice, here, at the cemetery," Kang volunteered. "It was after I saw the dean in his office for the last time."

"You did what?"

"You heard me right, Sergeant. It was two days before his body was found in that creek. When I read that in the paper, I was sick with fear that they might arrest me."

"You never told me that you went to see the dean two nights before he died."

"Of course I didn't," Kang said. "Why brag about it? But I'm telling you now! I'm not making it up."

"Go on, tell me more."

"It was the evening TV reran footage of the last day of the war. I had been miserable since my return home without my brother. What triggered my anger that night was the TV news: the scenes on the screen took me right back to the farming village where we lost many of our comrades, Sergeant.

"In one scene, there were thousands of Vietnamese refugees trying to board a U.S. troop ship anchored at the dock, but the American MPs with white armbands didn't let them. One young Vietnamese woman with a bundle on her head handed her baby wrapped in a blanket to an American soldier boarding the ship, calling him 'darling' and jabbering something, but the soldier disappeared into the vessel, making her weep.

"And in another scene, refugees were getting onto a fishing boat and a small airplane approached, shooting and killing the refugees. I wanted to see if Dean Dolan was watching the scenes I was watching. He's responsible for my brother's early death, you know, as well as 5,000 others killed in Vietnam.

"I still have the pistol I used in Vietnam, as you probably do too, Sergeant. I took it with me, just in case. I had no intention of killing the dean, of course; I just wanted to have a heart-to-heart conversation with him about allowing the government to send us to the country that was falling into communist hands. The College gate was closed, as I had expected, but the side door for the employees was still open. The building was dark, but Father Dolan's office was brightly lit. Following the light, I walked the dark corridor quietly. In front of his window, I could see him sitting at his double-sized wooden desk, scribbling something.

"I twisted the doorknob very gently and the door opened and I stepped in. There was the smell of whiskey, and I saw a suspicious bottle resting on the desk next to his left elbow. To my surprise, he didn't lift his head to see who had entered. But he said, 'Are you leaving now, Officer Lee?' He thought I was one of the security guards, can you imagine? I didn't say anything, knowing that he'd eventually see me standing there. I felt powerful, Sergeant. It was the same kind of feeling I had in Vietnam when I captured a sniper hiding in a vacant home and we hanged him on a Napa Tree, remember?

"I was right: Dean Dolan eventually lifted his face, and seeing me, his handsome American face turned pale. 'Kang Jung-soo…? Is that you?' he said.

"'Dean Dolan, it's been such a long time', I said as coldly as I could manage.

"'Please, have a seat,' he said, rising from the desk. 'I… I heard about your brother, Jung-hoon… I'm very sorry…'

"I thought I could spit at him, Sergeant! I wanted to tell him I didn't come to hear how sorry he was for my brother or the thousands of others killed in Vietnam. I wanted to tell him that I came to hear him say how he felt now after South Vietnam crumbled down and was about to vanish from the face of the world.

"But instead, I heard me say, 'Dear respectful Dean, I came to thank you for praying for us. Without your prayers, I might have died there, like 5,000 others.' Dolan's lips trembled as his gaze dropped to the papers he had been writing earlier. I heard his long sigh.

"'All my combat buddies who returned are grateful to you for your prayers as well, Dean Dolan, though some of them will never walk or carry their own children with their own arms. And some will spend the rest of their lives in a mental hospital…'

"'Please stop,' the Dean said, hitting his desk with his hand, startling me. I saw tears fill his eyes and then roll down his handsome face. In a trembling voice, he said, 'If I could change what I did three years earlier, I would. But it's too late…' He rambled on, saying that he had no other choice but to support the government policies. 'All foreign missionaries had to swear on paper when they entered the country that they'd respect and support the laws of the country. But,' he said, 'if you thought I blindly agreed with your president, you're wrong, Jung-soo. I cared for our students! Who has the wisdom of knowing the outcome of the war? No one does.'

"I wanted to laugh and scream at him, saying he bargained with our lives to make himself look good to our money-thirsty president, but my throat was tight and tears came to my eyes.

"Dean Dolan stood up and opened his desk drawer. He pulled out two plastic glasses. Then, he uncorked the bottle with his teeth and poured whiskey into the glasses, one after another. 'Here, Jung-soo,' he said, thrusting one glass towards me. 'Let's drink to all those who fought in the war for the better future of the world. I'm sure your brother is watching this in Heaven at this moment. Peace!'

"Angry, I pushed the glass away, spilling the liquid on his pants and on the floor. 'Drink it to your heart's content, Dean Dolan!' I yelled. Then I heard footsteps in the corridor and a man's voice saying, 'Are you alright, Dean Dolan?' I quickly crouched on the floor on the other side of the dean's desk, holding my breath.

"'Yes. I'm alright, Officer Lee!' Dolan said. 'I thought I heard voices. Who's with you?' said the guard. 'Oh, I was rehearsing my homily for Sunday. Maybe I was too loud. There's nothing to worry about, Officer Lee,' Dolan said.

"'Sorry to disturb you, Father Dolan,' said the guard. 'No problem at all. Are you about done for today?' Dolan asked. 'Not yet, sir. I'll be here for another hour or two because my replacement for the night just called and said that he'll be late in coming because of a traffic accident on the highway,' the guard said. 'I see. I'll be here for a while too. If you need to leave, please do so at any time,' Dolan responded. 'In that case, I'll go home, sir. See you in the morning,' the officer said and walked away.

"Father Dolan looked at me hunched on the floor. He seemed worried about me, Sergeant. He opened a drawer and produced a key. 'Why don't you go to the chapel and spend the night there?' he whispered. 'When the school opens in the

44

morning, it's safe to walk out without being noticed by the security officers on duty.'

"I thanked him and walked out of his office and hid in the chapel, Sergeant. He could have handed me to the security officer, but he did not. Then, two days later, I read in the newspaper that Dean Dolan had been drowned in a creek on the northern end of Seoul. I couldn't believe it. But who could have shot him in the back of his head, as the newspapers described?"

The sunlight had faded and now the sky was turning gray. Several crows sat on the heads of the statue of the soldiers and were squawking away, as if they had heard the two men's conversations.

After a long moment of silence, Kim said, "Jung-soo, what would you do if you were me? Would you meet the guy Father Patrick told me about?"

"I'd meet the guy. What was his name again?"

Chapter Five
Dean Dolan's Lifetime Possessions

On the following Saturday morning, Michael remembered his appointment with Father Patrick at Sonam College, the college his father supposedly had founded in the early 1960s and served as the dean for. He and Father Patrick were to visit Father Murphy, his father's successor. Michael wanted to see the school but wasn't eager to see the things his father used to own. *What am I going to do with his old watch, ring, diary, and the articles about him? Do I really want to read his diary?* It was great meeting Father Patrick and hearing about his father, not because his father had been a Catholic priest with an impressive reputation, but because he now had some idea where he had come from. But he wasn't ready to actually see and touch the things that had belonged to his dead father.

Seeing through the window that it was a sunny day with a clear blue sky, Michael toyed with the idea of jogging along the banks of the Han River and feeling free and strong before he'd find himself at the school and talking to his father's co-worker. About this time of the year, all sorts of wild birds from the wildlife sanctuary along the 38th Parallel, known as 'No Man's Land', would migrate to the Pacific for approaching winter, creating a spectacular scene in the air. The cranes with white napes or red crowns were his favorites. To observe these rare species with long legs and long, crooked necks, ecologists and bird scientists from all over the world visited Seoul, according to what he had read. *Why couldn't I go see them? Who could stop me?*

He rolled off his bed and rushed to the washroom. After brushing his teeth, he took a hot shower, changed into his jogging suit, put on his wool hat and sneakers, and ran out the door. The air was chilly on his face, but his spirit was free and exuberant. He jogged along the walking path that would lead him to the children's playground by the Han River on the other side of highway that had a gym set, swings, and a large sandbox, bordered by wooden benches. 20 minutes later, he was out of breath. He sat on a bench facing the river. The sun had risen, coloring the clouds in orange and yellow. The river's surface was shimmering gold liquid. The timing had been perfect, because a flock of about 30 large snow cranes with enormous white wings flew over him, squealing joyfully. They could be the ones that live along the DMZ in springtime but now were migrating to the Pacific. They could fly very high, about a mile high, from sea-level, he remembered reading about them. Poets and writers had described them as birds of wisdom and longevity, and some Buddhists called them 'birds of immortality'. How pleasant it was, he thought, facing the river on a calm morning like this. Though the current was moving in a dazzling speed towards the East Sea, the landscape was peaceful and its sounds gentle, as gentle as his mother's voice singing a lullaby in his ears when he was a small boy. *Will I ever see her?* he thought with longing. He wished he could stop his *life-clock* and freeze this moment forever.

At two that afternoon, Father Patrick and Michael met in the parking lot of Sonam College campus, in front of a white building with 'Administration' written in bold Korean letters.

Michael was bewildered at seeing such a large campus with many red brick buildings. *Is this what my own father built from scratch?*

"Before you meet Father Murphy," Father Patrick said after they exchanged short greetings. "I want you to know a few more things about him."

"Yes, Father."

As he led the way towards a tall white building, he said, "Though your father and Father Murphy worked harmoniously together for many years, they were very different types of men. Your father was a public figure and a man of ideas and dreams, but he wasn't detail-oriented. Father Murphy, on the other hand, is a scholar and a mathematician with crystal-clear memory. He can tell you a lot about your father."

"I'm a bit nervous about meeting him, Father."

"I know how you feel, but just think that you're meeting a kind and gentle old man who knew your father well. He'll not have any preoccupations about you or anyone for that matter. Trust me!"

"Thank you!" Michael had met Father Patrick only once, a few days earlier, but he felt he knew this priest, who exuded a certain authority yet was gentle and kind. What choice did he have but trust his words? As he followed Father Patrick, he found himself anticipating seeing inside this building that his father could have directed an architect to design and even coached him, giving the details. *Was the architect a Korean or an American?*

They climbed the stone steps leading to a square landing supported by tall white marble columns.

"Father Patrick!" a man's voice rang, at the same time an old American priest emerged from the door.

"Father Murphy, thank you for agreeing to meet with us."

"It's my pleasure, my old friend," Father Murphy said.

The two priests embraced.

"I'm always glad to see you, Patrick. You bring memories of our olden days!"

Michael found himself smiling; Father Murphy seemed like a kind grandpa he'd never had.

"James," Father Patrick said, calling Father Murphy by his first name, "I want you to meet Michael Hamil, the young man we spoke about."

Father Murphy embraced Michael in the same manner he had embraced Father Patrick—gently. "I'm glad to meet you, Michael. Hope to see you many more times."

"Same here, Father Murphy."

"Let's go inside, shall we?" the old priest said, motioning Michael to enter the door he had emerged from. As they passed the entrance and turned at the corner into a sun-lit corridor, Father Murphy turned to Michael and asked, "Is this your first visit to the College?"

"Yes."

"Then we should have you tour the school."

"A good idea," Father Patrick said. "I was going to show him around the campus on the way out."

"As you remember, Patrick, we still have a few photos of our first dean displayed on these two walls."

"I hoped so. Michael is eager to see them, I'm sure."

Against the well-polished wooden floor, their footsteps echoed. Windows on both sides of the corridor let in bright sunlight, making the white walls look bleached.

Father Murphy stopped in the middle of the hallway to face a framed black and white photo on the wall. "In this photo," he said, pointing, "your father is giving a speech at the dedication ceremony after the construction was done. It was spring of 1961. He was 36 years old at the time. Look at the men on the stage; sitting in the chairs in the center are the Korean bishop and his assistant—Bishop Noh and Father Baik—and the priests on the right are five American Jesuit professors from Milwaukee. And here, directly behind your father, are three Korean government officials we dealt with at the time."

Michael looked at the photo closely. This was the first time he was seeing his father's image, and he couldn't help but notice his heart beating faster. His father was tall and handsome, with dark, curly hair and light skin. He couldn't tell if he had blue eyes in this black and white photo. But as Father Patrick had mentioned, his father certainly had similar facial features as his own, except his father was a white man with lighter-colored hair, unlike himself, who had ginger-colored skin and straight jet-black hair.

"Your father was a gifted speaker," Father Murphy added, "besides being a man of ideas and a great diplomat."

Father Patrick said, "I'm not in this photo, Michael, because this was long before I joined the faculty."

"That's right," Father Murphy agreed. Turning to Father Patrick he said, "I believe you joined us four years later, in 1965, didn't you?"

"Yes. Back then the school only had four buildings—this Administration building, the Art and Science building, the School of Engineering and Technology, and the library. But now, it seems there are 20 buildings at least."

"We have 23 buildings all together, Patrick, including the gym," Father Murphy said with a certain pride. "Our students won two gold medals in the 24th Summer Olympics here in Seoul, one in swimming and another in marathon, and Sonam

College was voted the best college teaching arts and humanities among all Asian adult institutions. Would you believe it?"

"That's impressive!" Michael said.

Father Murphy moved a few steps in the same direction and stopped in front of another framed photo. "Here, your father is having dinner with the president of South Korea, President Park, and the cabinet members. He often served as a mediator whenever the Korean president had difficulties with the U.S. ambassador named Muccio. The president didn't speak any English, and Muccio was known for his arrogance against Koreans. No wonder why Koreans described him as 'a Yankee sticking his long nose into Korean affairs'," he laughed.

Father Patrick too laughed.

Michael didn't laugh. "I didn't know anything about my father," he confessed. "Seeing him in these photos makes me feel I'm actually meeting him. Thank you, Father Murphy."

"You're most welcome, Michael," the old priest said and patted his shoulder.

Michael coughed softly as if trying to control his emotion. "Without your father's courage and ingenuity," Father Murphy continued, "Sonam College wouldn't exist today and we wouldn't have all those buildings out there nor would we have more than 30,000 students."

"Where is my father buried?" Michael asked.

"Behind that hill," Father Murphy said, lifting his left arm towards east. "He's among the dozen American missionaries buried there. We'll take you there, if you want."

"I'd like it very much, but at another time, Father."

"Very well! Let me know when you want to visit."

Then, they entered a large office with a bookcase against one wall, a display case showing framed certificates and gold trophies; and a small ceramic nativity-set on the opposite wall. Against the window facing the parking lot stood a flagpole holding the familiar red, white, and blue flag. "This room once belonged to your father," Father Murphy said, "but it's now my office. We added another wing facing the pond, and the dean's office moved there. Most of the things in here—bookcases, cabinets, and wall hangings—were here when your father used this office."

"Thank you for telling me that," Michael said, looking around.

"Do you like it?" Father Murphy asked, smiling.

"Very much, Father! I never dreamed that I'd someday stand in an office that once belonged to my father. It means so much to me." He looked at a painting of a cowboy hung on a wall and said, "He must have liked cowboys, I imagine."

"Yes, he did," Father Murphy said. "He loved reading books, but in the evenings, he enjoyed watching cowboy movies. Patrick," he said, turning to Father Patrick standing next to him, "tell Michael about the campus festival we had here after you joined us."

Father Patrick's face lit with a boyish smile. "Our dean had many talents, Michael," he said, trying to hide his excitement. "But on the campus festival day, he was John Wayne himself on a big screen, riding a horse around the campus. We priests also dressed like someone of our choice; for instance, Father Murphy dressed as Abraham Lincoln; Father Mitchell, the English teacher, was Uncle Sam; and I an American policeman. But your father was the best, because he truly loved being a cowboy."

"Did Korean people come to the festival?" Michael asked.

"Thousands of them, including children," Father Patrick said. "It was your father's idea to introduce 20th century America to the Korean people, who were still far behind civilization, in our opinion. All sorts of carnival equipment were brought into the campus, and vendors selling American food—hotdogs, hamburgers, and French fries—each set up a booth. Imagine, most Koreans had never tasted ice cream before the Korean War! The Koreans, both men and women, were still wearing loosely fitting ancient clothing—particularly men with funny-looking black hats made of stiff, wiry material—and still regarded the Chinese sage Confucius as their eternal master. Anyway, the festival was a grand success, with jazz music blasting through the speakers and young men and young women dancing together while their parents and grandparents clicked their tongues in disgust. That was the beauty of the festival; we created friends and enemies at the same time!" he laughed.

"I wish I had been there, Fathers," Michael said. "It sounds like a great opportunity for the native people to see what the U.S. was like."

"You bet, it was. The newspapers wrote about it, and many Koreans parents came to the school just to find out what it looked like."

Murphy said, "Michael, ask me anything you want to know about your father and I will tell you all I know about him. He and I worked together peacefully, like two hands working together, though we occasionally had different ways of handling things. I surely miss him."

Michael didn't know what to ask about his father he had never met. And Father Murphy was a stranger to him. An awkward silence fell in the room as Michael dropped his gaze onto his hands on his lap.

"If you don't have any question, then, I have one for you," Murphy said.

"Yes, Father."

"Father Patrick told me that you returned to Korea three years earlier to live here permanently. This was, in my understanding, after you'd participated the Adoptee Home Visit Program two years ago, am I correct?"

"Yes, Father."

"How did you find out about that program? I'm curious. Did some Koreans where you lived tell you about it?"

"It was sort of a surprise when I heard about it. I was a high school dropout then and was working at a fast food restaurant selling all kinds of Asian food—Korean barbeque called *Bul-go-ghi,* Japanese *sushi and sashmi*, and Vietnamese noodle soups called *Pho.* The owners were a Korean couple who spoke bare-minimum English. One day, a well-dressed Korean woman came for lunch, and seeing me clearing dishes and wiping the tables, asked me if I were half-Korean. I said yes, a bit surprised that she could notice my Korean facial features. She acted delighted. 'I was looking for you,' she said, in a cheerful tone of voice.

"'Looking for me?' I asked. 'Yes,' she said. She told me the Korean Embassy in Chicago sent her to find as many Korean men and women who were adopted to American

52

families as children and lived in the U.S. and encourage them to visit their motherland that summer, all expenses paid.

"I was more embarrassed than I was glad for my chance to visit what she called my 'motherland', because the owners and two other employees I worked with didn't know that I was an orphan. And here she was, talking loudly about my shameful past as a 'reject' and asking me whether I wanted to visit my 'motherland'.

"I said nothing and kept doing what I was doing. She didn't leave me alone. She took out a small booklet from her bag and handed it to me. The front cover had bold print that read 'Welcome Home' in front of what looked like a flag that had red and blue inside a circle in the center and some black lines at its four corners. She said, 'Take it home with you and read it. Again, it doesn't cost you anything, not even a dime. Your motherland invites you *home,* where you were born, and all six international adoption agencies in Seoul are paying for your travel expenses. Why not take the chance and meet other young people like yourself, coming from all over the world?' She looked dead serious.

"I took the brochure home and looked at it from the front cover and back, many times. The thought that I might find my mother caused me to lose sleep. Yet, it took me two whole years to finally make up my mind to come, and I'm glad I did."

Father Murphy said, "I'm glad for you too. That experience must have been positive for you. Otherwise, you wouldn't have moved here to make your home. As I said earlier, I want you to come see me as many times as you wish."

"James," Father Patrick interrupted. "As I said on the phone, you once told me you were keeping Father Dolan's belongings and that I could come get them whenever I wanted. I brought Michael here because he's the rightful owner of his father's belongings."

"Thanks for reminding me." Father Murphy walked towards the bookcase against the opposite wall and reached for a wooden box at the top the size of a briefcase.

Seeing that Father Murphy couldn't quite reach it and worried that the old man might fall on the hardwood floor, Michael rose to help. But Murphy got it, and turning, he said, "Oh, here you are!" surprised that Michael stood behind him.

"This is yours. Your father will be glad that you have his things."

Michael took it. The box felt lighter in his arms than it looked when Father Murphy lowered it from the top of the bookcase. "Father Murphy, thank you!"

Chapter Six
Union of Father and Son

It was late afternoon by the time Michael and Father Patrick parted with Father Murphy. The view of the Han River and mountains ahead was blanketed by white clouds as they walked out of the Administration building together. "Michael, why don't you come to my place? We can look through the items together, if you don't mind?"

"I was thinking that too, Father," Michael said. "It's a bit overwhelming to think that I'll soon be touching and looking through things that belonged to my father I never met. I don't know what to expect. I'm not all that exited, to tell you the truth."

"It's all set then. Drive carefully," Father Patrick said. "About this time of the day, the traffic is a nightmare."

"I'll be careful. I'll see you soon."

Michael loaded the box on the backseat of his Hyundai Sonata and followed Father Patrick as he drove out of the parking lot. The traffic was indeed a nightmare. Not only were there a stream of passenger cars and a few trucks he often saw on a freeway during the day, there were also many semi-trucks and construction vehicles ahead of him, blocking his view. In five minutes, he lost sight of Father Patrick's old Toyota in the dense traffic.

By the time Michael exited the freeway and turned in the direction of the church, the sun was setting and he was hungry and exhausted. As expected, Father Patrick stood on the front steps of the church as he had the first time they met a few days earlier. Michael parked, in the same spot, got out, and retrieved the box from the backseat

"Do you need help with it?" Father Patrick asked, standing behind him.

"No, thank you, Father. It's not heavy at all."

"I'm glad you made it here okay."

"I am, too."

They walked to Father Patrick's office, through the church as they had before, to a room with the sign 'Pastor's Office' on the door. Inside, Father cleared the coffee table by pushing off a magazine and newspapers and Michael gently set the box on it.

"Michael, you must be hungry. I have some leftover macaroni and cheese from yesterday."

"Father, thank you. But I don't feel like eating anything now."

"How about something to drink?"

"No thank you, Father."

Michael removed the lid of the box, and turning it upside down, he dumped the contents onto the table. A stack of letters bound by a thin cord, a notebook with a blue cover, a black book titled '*Divine Office*', and a small leather pouch landed on the table. A musty smell rose into the air. Sitting on the floor, Michael opened the leather bag first and produced a whitish bamboo comb. He took it to his face and sniffed. "This is my father's smell," he said, smiling like a small child full of curiosity.

Father Patrick laughed. "Can you see his fingerprints on it?"

"I wish I could," he said, running his fingers from one end to another.

"What else is in the pouch?"

"A can of shoe polish, a tube of hand cream or hair lotion, and a gold ring…" He then lifted several toy plastic handcuffs from the pouch. "What are these?"

Father Patrick's eyes widened. "Let me see," he said. Taking one of the plastic objects from Michael, he examined it, turning it this way and that. "Do you remember the campus carnival we talked to you about earlier today?"

"Yes."

"When I played an American cop one year, I bought these at a toy store. I pretended I was arresting the rambunctious kids making so much noise with these and they loved it. Their parents loved it more, actually. I never thought your father would keep them with his other belongings."

Michael's expression turned playful for a moment but didn't last. He looked sad as he said, "I wish I'd met him…" He untied the bundle of letters and looked through them carefully. He lifted one envelope, saying, "Father, he wrote to me!"

"He did?"

"Yes. Look at this; he wrote on the envelope, 'To my son I'll never meet'."

"He must have written it after he learned of your birth. Go on, read it, if you don't mind!"

Michael opened it and fell silent as his eyes glued on the paper, his lips moving in silence. The wall clock tick-tocked and the voices of vendors from the street below suddenly became audible.

Michael unexpectedly handed the letter to Father Patrick, saying, "Please read it, Father."

"Me? Are you sure?"

"Yes, please. It's something I can't keep to myself. I want someone to know what he must have felt when he wrote this, knowing that he'd never meet me. Please, Father, go on and read it."

Father Patrick took it and read it:

To my son I'll never meet:

Perhaps no other father ever wrote to his son the way I'm writing to you now. All I can ask is for you to forgive me for bringing you to life and walking away as soon as I was aware. I'm such a hypocrite, Son. How many couples I have blessed and joined in the sacrament of matrimony! How many newborns I have baptized in God's name! And how many mothers I have congratulated at the news that they were pregnant! I even thanked the Almighty for choosing me for His instrument for blessing the newborns… But for my own, I couldn't face the reality and sent your mother, a student at the college I've established, away when she broke the news to me. That was more than four years earlier, Son.

But yesterday, I read your mother's long hand-written letter, describing her pain and sorrow of taking you to the orphanage the adoption agency had recommended. What words can describe how I feel now. I'm no better than a cow on the field that doesn't know he has his offspring nearby and peacefully grazes on the grass. I detest myself, Son.

I have caused you and your mother so much pain in order to keep my face as the American Jesuit who founded the first Catholic college in Korea. Yes, I worked very hard to be who I've become today. I thought God sent me here to do His grand work. I lived with that sense of greatness and pride, and when I learned of your upcoming birth, I couldn't deal with it. Let me tell you my side of the story:

After Sonam College was established, with only a hundred students and with the main building standing, the enrollment almost doubled every year. The people I worked with praised me for what I had done. Even the South Korean government under President Park thought Sonam College was a godsend. The president himself invited me to the presidential mansion to praise me for the College and occasionally asked me to help him deal with the stiff-necked American ambassador looking for dirt to report to the U.S. government. Fifteen years later, when the school was growing beyond my expectation, I learned the unbelievable truth, I caused a conception; I couldn't accept it. It could perhaps be compared to a pilot flying a jet about to crash into a swamp 10,000 feet below.

Son, life isn't yours to keep and enjoy; it's given to you for a purpose. Do not make the same mistake I made, but accept the cross He gives you to carry. Unless you do what's given to you, you'll never understand Jesus' death and resurrection. May God bless you always.

Your father, John Dolan, May 30, 1975

Michael noticed Father Patrick's brown eyes filling with tears as he returned the letter, without a word.

"Father, I'm curious about how he died."

"Why?"

"Because in the letter, he was full of remorse about the way he treated my mother and me."

"It's understandable, isn't it?"

"I suppose, but it makes me wonder whether he ended his own life, because, soon afterwards, he was found in a remote creek somewhere, as you've told me."

"Michael, my feeling is he didn't do that. But who can tell for sure? The only person who can shed some light on your father's death is Dr. Kim Youn-gill, one of my old former students who's now a well-known medical doctor here in Seoul. He identified your father's remains while he was an intern in the forensic lab at Seoul University Medical Center. I'll contact him if you want to meet him."

"Yes, I do. On the other hand, I want to know if Dr. Kim liked my father when he was a student at Sonam College. I don't want to meet him if he hated my father."

"I'll let him tell you about that himself. Most students respected their dean until the government deployed thousands of young men to Vietnam to fight, and your father complied with the law." Father Patrick took his cell phone from his pocket and punched the keys.

* * *

An hour later, a gray-haired Korean man wearing glasses with a thick black-frame walked into the room, looking tired. With a quick nod to Father Patrick, he stared at Michael without a word. Father Patrick said, "Dr. Kim, this is my new friend Michael I mentioned earlier and Michael, meet Dr. Kim, my old student who's now a distinguished medical doctor."

The two men shook hands, Michael still sitting on the floor. Dr. Kim sat on the sofa, facing Father Patrick.

"You do look like Father Dolan quite a bit, Michael, tall and with that Irish good-look."

"Do you think so?" Michael said, blushing.

"Yes, very much. Father Patrick said you moved to Seoul about three years ago. Your Korean is wonderful!"

"Thanks."

Dr. Kim looked at the items spread on the coffee table before him—letters, a notebook, plastic handcuffs, and more letters. "Are these Father Dolan's?" he asked Father Patrick.

"Yes. Michael and I picked up the box you see on the floor early this afternoon from Father Murphy. I told Michael that you were the person who examined Father Dolan after he was found in the creek. Michael was wondering if Father Dolan might have ended his life with his own hands."

"Why do you think that?" Kim asked.

"Because, in his letter that I just read, he was apologetic and remorseful about how he treated my mother and me. Unless he was planning to end his life, why would a man write a letter to his son, saying, 'The son I'll never meet', and call himself a 'hypocrite'?"

Dr. Kim adjusted his thick black glass-frame and said, "The pieces of the puzzle still don't fit together about whether he killed himself or someone did a clean job of him and vanished. Interestingly, the day he was found in that creek was a month after the Vietnam War ended. Some of us veterans are still wondering the same question: did Dean Dolan end his own life from the guilt of sending us to Vietnam or did someone kill him for some reason? To answer your question, Michael, a dead body doesn't always give a clue as to whether they ended their own life or someone murdered them. But, in my opinion, he was murdered and I reported it that way. He couldn't have handcuffed himself and shot himself in the back of his head and jumped into the river, too. Such things don't happen."

"Then why did he write this letter to me?"

"Who can tell?" Kim said in a brotherly manner. "He might have thought about ending his life when he wrote it but changed his mind at the last minute. But he acknowledged you, believing that someday the letter would reach you. Dean Dolan was not an ordinary man, I can tell you that."

"Would you please elaborate it? In what way?"

"Let's leave it at that, Michael," Father Patrick said with authority almost abruptly. "If we keep digging, we'll find more mysteries that'll send us into spiral of imagination and insanity. And Dr. Kim is tired after a long day in operating rooms at the hospital, and you're tired, too!" He then said to Dr. Kim, "Thank you for coming, Dr Kim!"

Chapter Seven
Father Dolan's Diary

Returning to his apartment in Shinchon that night, Michael had enough courage to open his father's diary, a small book the size of his palm with a black cover. The first page read:

September 16, 1955.

Finally, my companion Father Tom Gregory, SJ., and I arrived in Seoul and settled in the guesthouse in Myongdong Cathedral. The mountains are bare. People look primitive in their loosely fitting traditional garments—men and women both. But old men wear tall black hats made of stiff hemp. They look strange and curious about us westerners.

On the way into the town from Kimpo airport in a taxicab, we were shocked at seeing the skeletons of buildings and homes damaged during the three-year war earlier in the decade. I wish the debris—burned bricks, splinters of wood, and torn, discolored clothes—could tell us who destroyed them—the Russian MiGs or our U.S. bombers—but they don't. We can only imagine what the war had been like.

This country is blessed with tall mountains, clear streams, and a sapphire-blue sky when it doesn't rain. But during the monsoon season that lasts weeks, you'd feel that the people of this tiny nation must have angered the Almighty somehow, because the thunder sounds as if boulders on mountaintops are wreaking havoc below.

The nation's earlier tragedy before the war is evident. Mountains are bald, because the Japanese, who ruled the country for 40 years until they surrendered to the allied forces in 1945, stole everything from the Koreans—trees, manpower, their identity as Koreans, and natural treasures such as gold, silver, iron, tungsten, copper, and more.

Yet, Koreans are humble: they always bow to any Westerner, mostly Americans, showing appreciation for helping them gain freedom from their communist invaders that mowed them down with Russian tanks. But not all Westerners are here to help them; many came to look for fortune, selling western clothes, food, and daily essentials such as hairdryers, radios, and furniture, anything they don't have, which is a lot. And most of these Western merchants are rude, stiff-necked, and arrogant to the Koreans.

Is it because they are taller and bigger than the natives? Is it because the Koreans can't speak English? Is it because they know nothing about Korea's 5,000 years of written history and rich culture that respects elders? I'm embarrassed about my own American brothers and sisters' superiority shown to the poor yet wise people of this ancient country.

We'll soon have to find a home for us. We're thinking about renting a room and an office from Ewha Women's College, established by the U.S. Methodist Episcopalian Church, headed by Mary F. Scranton, in the late 19th century.

Almighty, here I am, in Korea.
Speak to me, Lord, in my heart
In a way I can understand
Your servant is awake and listening

Michael skipped a few pages and read on.

August 5, 1961.
We're well-established now. Two buildings have been erected and are operating, with a dozen administrative staff, six professors, while construction workers are still digging, drilling and pounding. Often, we six priests get invited to Korean families, thanks to the Benedictine Sisters who operate a health clinic in a neighborhood near the Central Train Station.

62

One family we've visited a few times is the Suhs'. Both parents are devout Catholics and their oldest son, a seminarian in Seoul, is accepted to a well-respected seminary in Paris and will soon leave the country. He will be the first Korean man who will no doubt be ordained in a most prestigious Roman Catholic Church in the Church's history in a few years. The second son is already in Germany, in Achen, studying economics. Their three younger sisters are in music school, two pianists and one cellist, all wanting to study abroad after graduation.

Another middle-aged couple we know have sent all their four sons to the U.S., two studying engineering, another medicine, another international law.

I see the future of South Korea through the minds of these young Koreans—some already abroad and some about to leave. God willing, 20 years from now, this country will shed her poverty and war-ashes and dust and shine above many others that are far ahead of her in civilization today."

Opening to the middle section of the diary, Michael read:

June 16, 1970.

Today, tens of thousands demonstrated against the government sending Korean troops to Vietnam. Some of our students were beaten up so badly that they were unrecognizable. If the students continue to demonstrate, more students will be hurt, even fatally shot by the Special Forces. Already more than 200 students in Seoul lost their lives by the bullets shot by the policemen whose primary goals were to protect their citizens. I'm helpless as a Christian missionary who signed an agreement with the government to never speak ill of the nation and support the government, even when the public speaks against it. We, the American Jesuit missionaries, didn't expect such a disaster could happen here nearly 20 years ago when we arrived. We only dwelled on feeding the hungry, clothing them, sheltering them, and teaching them Christ's love. And now we're betrayers in the eyes of the public, particularly when the students are forced to leave their country to fight for the people of Vietnam. I wonder how many will return to see their family members again.

Almighty, why are you hiding Your face from us?

All I see is darkness.

Students are beaten or dying by policemen who swore in oath to protect them.

Yet I play mute, deaf, and blind.

Lift Your rod of justice and tell them who you are. Tell them to fear you! Turning still more pages, Michael found that some pages were missing. He had no choice but to tread the last pages.

March 31, 1975.

Dear Mother,

Your letter found me at the lowest point of my entire 50 years. You were the captain of my life vessel, named 'John Dolan', during all my school days, including my seminary years and beyond. You took charge of me in every aspect of life. With your encouragement and beliefs in me, I achieved a great height. Thanks to you, I embarked on my journey to this unknown place named Korea from San Francisco in 1955 with another Jesuit. We dealt with obstacles and unkind climates, and after six years, built the first Catholic college for Korean men and women on 5,000 acres of land overlooking the Han River, as it stands now. But 20 years after my first day here, the words in your letter whip me like bamboo whips that Koreans use on troublemakers. I'm sorry I revealed that I unintentionally fathered a child. I could have hidden it from you, Mother. But I couldn't, because I never lied to you about anything and I don't want to now. I looked myself square in the eyes in order to do 'right' from the 'wrong' I caused. I want to leave the priesthood and shed my pride as the founder and the dean of the College and embrace the life of a humble father and husband to the student who conceived my child.

But it was a harsh blow to you. I don't know how to undo what I've done, nor do I want to continue this double-life as a successful Jesuit missionary and dean and founder of the College that made all my Jesuit brothers in

Milwaukee proud, but I am a broken man. When I'm alone with the Almighty, the answer is clear: 'John Dolan, I've died on the cross to forgive the sins of mankind; I abide in you and you abide in me.'

But for you, Mother, my stepping down from my position is an insult to your pride as my mother. I know you've given me much—as a single mom. When I'm alone, I see myself as a beast I've read about in Greek mythology— a man with the body of a horse. I'm divided. I want to keep being your son and do what I've been doing, ignoring my inner struggle, but in the depth of my soul, I can not. I'm a sinner in the eyes of God. I'm in fear of His judgment for abandoning my son and his mother both. I feel a feeble joy imagining myself holding my child in one arm and his mother in another; no glory, no recognition for what I've done in the past but accepting my situation whole-heartedly as a humble man capable of loving his child and a woman he innocently fell in love with at his most vulnerable moment.

Mother, please look at me as I am now. Don't see me as your son, who obeyed you all his life and satisfied your ego as a triumphant mother. God wants us to be humble as He was before His Father!

John Dolan

Michael's hand trembled when he closed the book. This was totally unexpected. At the same time, he didn't want to remember his father's bitterness toward his mother when Michael himself didn't know where his mother was and how to find her. He placed the diary back in the box, closed and kissed it, before putting the box on the top shelf of his bookcase, at the corner, never to open it again.

Chapter Eight
Charlie

Michael woke up to loud knocking on his apartment door. He had gone to bed late the night before after reading his father's diary. His head throbbed as he rose from bed and asked, "Who's there?"

"*Ummmm!* It's me, Charlie."

Charlie? Michael hurried to the door and opened it. Charlie must have been leaning on the door, because when the door opened, he collapsed onto the floor like timber, blood oozing from his left temple and his topcoat showing blotches of darkened blood.

"Charlie, what happened to you?"

"*Ummmm...* Some Korean boys attacked me."

"What Korean boys? Where?"

"The rough-looking guys at the bar... The same bar where we used to hang out after our concerts."

"You mean at Sparrow's Lounge near the New Age Theater?"

"Yeah. Remember the boys who always made jokes about my color?"

Michael remembered. There had been four teenage boys who were drinking beer one night when Charlie and he had walked in. Seeing Charlie, one of them said, "Do you see that the room got darker now?" and giggled.

"Yeah, the ceiling light suddenly dimmed," said another. Amazingly, Charlie paid no attention to them and nothing ugly ever happened.

"Did you go there by yourself tonight?" Michael asked.

"I did. I thought they'd leave me alone. But they didn't. One of them came to the table where I sat, with the smell of beer in his breath, and sniffed around me, saying, 'Hey,

African, you smell like a buffalo,' and his gang laughed. I couldn't ignore him. To teach him a lesson, I pushed my glass of water towards him, spilling water on his pants. That's when the rest of them charged at me, hitting my back with their elbows or whistling in my ear and pulling my hair too. They were rats for sure."

"Didn't the owner do anything? Did he just stand there and watch when they behaved like that?"

"The Korean grandpa yelled at the boys to leave or he'd call the police, but the boys didn't stop. Finally, I stood up and punched them. I knocked two boys onto the floor and was still fighting when a tall and broad-shouldered man wearing an apron emerged from the kitchen and said to me, 'Leave or I'll cook you alive, *Gorilla!*' He was holding a wide kitchen knife, Michael, and he called me *Gorilla*. He took the boys' side. I couldn't believe it. Scared, I left instantly. 'Don't come back!' the man yelled. I passed the poorly lit parking lot and then walked towards the main road. Tall trash dumpsters were lined up on one side, and as I passed them, dark figures flew out from behind like flying monkeys I saw on TV. They were all Korean boys."

Michael checked the bruises on Charlie's face and his other wounds and told him he needed medical care. Charlie nodded, and Michael called an ambulance. While waiting for the ambulance to arrive, Michael picked up his guitar from its stand by his desk and played the melody of *The Promised Land in the Far East* that Charlie himself had composed and their band performed many times. Charlie buried his face in his hands and cried.

Michael too cried.

A faint siren wailing outside alerted them both, but Michael kept playing until a loud banging confirmed that the ambulance had arrived.

Michael opened the door with the guitar in one hand.

A policeman and two men in white gowns carrying a stretcher, one on each end, entered.

"We're here to pick up a man bleeding from a gang attack," one of the men in white gown said.

Michael stepped aside to let them in. While the medic checked Charlie's vital signs, the policeman, in his mid-30s,

67

asked Charlie questions. *Your name? Who beat you? Where? What time? Can you describe any of the assailants?*

Charlie told the same story he had told Michael, and when it was done, he obediently lay on the stretcher as told. As the medics carried him out of the room, Michael hurriedly put on his topcoat and followed them. While the medics loaded Charlie onto the ambulance, Michael asked if he could come along, describing himself as Charlie's friend. The driver said yes and he boarded, squeezing himself in the narrow space between the policeman, who sat in a padded seat next to the back door, and Charlie lying in the stretcher on the other side. The ambulance snaked through the streets, its lights flashing and siren wailing.

W*hy did Charlie have to be treated like this because of his color?* Michael himself had it rough in Austin, Texas, as a youngster who was half-Korean, half-American. But seeing Charlie lying next to him, with bruises on his face, in this ambulance, angered him more than when he himself had been ridiculed by rough boys in Austin. And some Korean people noticed his not-so-Korean facial features here in his second home in Korea too.

In the ER, Michael signed a dozen papers for Charlie as his guardian so that Charlie could be treated. Neither Charlie nor he had Korean citizenship yet, so they were not eligible for medical insurance, Michael told the administration clerk. Soon, Charlie was pushed into an operation room.

After waiting more than two hours, Michael was relieved to know that Charlie's injuries weren't too serious and he wouldn't have to pay anything. The old doctor with a balding head said, "He'll be sleeping most of today and tomorrow. If he has a reaction to the medications we gave, like fever, rash, or vomiting, please let us know. Otherwise, after two or three days, he can go back to his normal activities."

The front desk clerk called a taxicab for them and they returned to Michael's studio apartment. Charlie insisted on going to his apartment, but Michael didn't allow him. What if those ill-bred boys were waiting for him? "You're safer here than at your own place for tonight," Michael said.

"Thanks, Michael," Charlie said in a subdued voice. "The truth is, I don't want to be alone at my place."

"I'm glad you'll stay! You can use my bed and I'll sleep on the sofa," Michael said.

"Hey, when I get better, I'm going to learn Taekwondo so no hoodlum can bother me."

"We can talk about it tomorrow. The doctor said you need to rest plenty."

Charlie didn't argue.

As the doctor had predicted, Charlie slept soundly that night and most of the following day. Michael had brought food from the market a block away and they had late lunch. Charlie's face was still puffy and bruised, but his expression was brighter, showing that he had recovered from the trauma. Before leaving the next day, Charlie confessed, "Michael, thanks again for all you've done for me. You're my brother I never had." He then gave Michael a bearhug and said, "See you at rehearsal."

Chapter Nine
Reunion of Mother and Son

As Michael was changing his bedsheets after Charlie left, the phone rang.

He picked up the receiver. "Hello?"

"Michael, I have both good news and bad news for you. Are you ready?" Father Patrick's voice said. Before Michael could respond, he said, "We found your mother! But she's in a hospital."

Michael sat on the bed, holding the phone against his ear. "Where is she, Father?"

"In a U.S. military cancer clinic that treats victims poisoned by dangerous chemicals. As you might be aware, after the Vietnam War ended, the American military dumped hazardous chemicals in Korean waterways. It was big news for many years."

He'd read about it in a Korean newspaper. People collected signatures on the street, petitioning America to take responsibility for dumping millions of gallons of defoliant Agent Orange in the southeastern part of South Korea, near the U.S. military settlement.

"I've read about it Father. But why is she there, in the clinic?" Michael fought not to panic.

"Sister Angela located her through her network of nurses and doctors. Do you remember the Sister named Angela I'd told you about on the first day we met?"

"Of course. She's the one who found out about me singing at New Age Theater with my group, isn't she?"

"Yes. Sister Angela and I met her doctor yesterday."

"You did? Why didn't you let me come with you yesterday?"

70

"Michael, Sister Angela wanted to know if the woman named *Maria Hyon* is the same person as your mother, Min-sook Hyon. Sister Angela is extremely cautious, and I don't blame her. That's why she had me come with her to confirm first, that Maria Hyon is indeed your mother, before breaking the news to you. Your mother must have changed her name some time ago."

"How was she yesterday?"

"We didn't meet her in person, Michael," Father Patrick said. "We only saw her through a window during the patients' lunch break. She looked pale and was in a wheelchair, but her mind seemed alert; she was conversing with other patients."

"Why is she in a wheelchair? Does Sister Angela know how she ended up there and when?" Michael asked in a demanding tone of voice.

"Sister Angela didn't tell me much, other than what I told you, Michael," Father Patrick said in a defensive voice.

"You should ask her doctor when you see her."

"When can I see her, Father?"

"Is this Thursday soon enough for you?"

"Thursday is two days from today!" Michael heard the sharp edges in his voice. "Why can't I see her sooner?"

"Michael, that's not my decision, okay?" Father Patrick said. "That's the day Dr. Yoon, her counselor, will have her in her office."

"What time on Thursday?"

* * *

Two days later, Father Patrick and Michael headed to the Eastern Rehab Hospital, located in the southern part of Seoul in Yongsan District, not far from the U.S. military headquarters. Father Patrick insisted on driving, saying he was more accustomed to driving on Korean highways than Michael. In the lobby, Father Patrick talked to the receptionist about their appointment and the receptionist called Dr. Yoon on the phone.

Two minutes later, a slender woman in her early 50s, in a white coat, wearing glasses, came to greet them. She then led them into a room with a large picture window facing a classroom. There were two dozen old women in bluish hospital

71

gowns sitting on benches, forming a half-circle. Before them stood a young Korean nurse, holding an open book and talking.

"They're in a group session," Dr. Yoon explained. "They're learning how to combat negative thoughts from our instructor. Can you see that only a few ladies are paying attention to their instructor?"

Michael observed the patients closely and agreed with the doctor. Some old ladies were asleep, their heads lowered the way flowers in a vase did when they withered. Others were talking with their seat partners; and one lady was knitting with two long needles and a ball of yellow yarn, paying no attention to their instructor.

"Dr. Yoon, do you see my mother in there?" Michael asked, his eyes glued to the picture window.

"See the lady in a wheelchair looking out the window, separated from the group?"

"Why isn't she with the rest of them? And what happened to her head… She's almost bald."

Father Patrick coughed into his hands, uncomfortable. "Michael, I should have told you more about her health when I broke the news, but I couldn't. She's in an advanced stage of cancer."

"What? She isn't dying, is she?"

Father Patrick looked at Dr. Yoon for help.

"No, she isn't dying today or tomorrow," Dr. Yoon said in a business-like manner. "But we don't know if she could be here next year."

"How long has she been ill like this?" Michael asked.

"About ten years. I helped her to be admitted to the hospital. That was when U.S. forces reluctantly acknowledged that a large amount of leftover pesticides, herbicides, and solvents that they used in the Vietnam War were dumped in Korean soil or creeks after the war ended, saying that the chemicals were not harmful to humans or animals. But with time, the American servicemen who buried around 600 barrels of toxic materials in Korea, stepped forward, revealing that their contact with the deadly poison had caused serious health problems—blindness, liver failure, cancer, and even death. The U.S. government then meekly acknowledged the harmful effects of coming into contact with the chemicals or drinking contaminated water. Many Koreans who lived in the area where the chemicals were dumped or buried came forward, too, each with a story supporting the American servicemen's claims. Some victims were children. Parents reported deformed children or babies that died at birth."

"Wow, I didn't know any of what you're saying," Michael said.

"The sad part was: Americans wouldn't treat just anyone who claimed they had consumed poisonous water. The patients had to prove that their symptoms were from consuming contaminated water and that they lived in an affected area. And in some cases, they had to provide a doctor's written note stating that they had symptoms caused by toxic chemicals U.S forces discarded near where they lived."

"How did my mother figure that she might be a victim of chemicals the U.S. military dumped in Korea?"

"When she came to me," Yoon said, "she was a nightclub pianist at the military base. She complained that she couldn't perform anymore because of extreme fatigue, fever, and headaches. I backed her theory, and she was admitted here. Soon, she lost the ability to play piano completely, because, in addition to her initial symptoms, her vision got poor and she lost weight. Now, she can't even walk."

"She certainly looks frail," Michael said in a congested voice.

"She looked much worse two years ago," Dr. Yoon said. "At least her condition stabilized, except for being confined to a wheelchair. Others have more serious symptoms, Mr. Hamil. See the lady on her left side? She lost the ability to speak and her left side is paralyzed. Your mother still has clear memories and her brain functions are almost normal."

"I want to meet my mother, Dr. Yoon," Michael said. "Will you let me see her today?"

"Yes, you'll meet her today," Dr. Yoon said in an assuring manner. "This session will end in about ten minutes and I'll have a nurse bring her to my office so you can meet with her. She might get quite emotional."

"That will make two of us!"

Dr. Yoon led Michael and Father Patrick to her office around the corner. "Please come in and have a seat at that table by the window," she pointed.

Father Patrick and Michael seated themselves, facing one another. The sunlight entering from the window was warm and bright.

"Would you like a cup of coffee, gentlemen?" Dr. Yoon asked.

"No thanks," Father Patrick said.

"Me neither," said Michael.

Dr. Yoon sat behind her cluttered desk, facing the door, and rearranged it while waiting.

A buzzing noise outside the door confirmed that the session had just ended. Two minutes later, a drone of a wheelchair in motion outside the door alerted them.

Michael coughed nervously into his hands.

Father Patrick straightened his Roman collar.

Dr. Yoon said, "Please, gentlemen, be as casual as you can manage, so that my patient won't be frightened."

A tall nurse opened the door and pushed a wheelchair into the room. In it was the frail-looking woman with sunken eyes they had seen earlier through the picture window. Now, she was attached to an oxygen tank, mounted on the back of her wheelchair, through a clear tube. She looked nervous, her eyes shifting. The nurse said to the old woman, "Have a good visit with your counsellor, Auntie Hyon. I'll come and get you when you're done, okay?" With a quick nod to Dr. Yoon, the nurse left.

Dr. Yoon said, "You look good, Miss Hyon. How are you feeling today?"

"I'm fine, thank you," Hyon said mechanically with a frail voice.

Dr. Yoon got behind the wheelchair and moved it next to her desk, with the patient facing her. "How did you like the class today, Miss Hyon?" she said as she seated herself back in her chair.

"It was boring," Hyon blurted out. It seemed as though she had not noticed the two men in the room. She squinted in the bright sunlight coming through the window.

Father Patrick observed Michael, whose eyes were glued to his mother.

Dr. Yoon asked, "Tell me, Miss Hyon, why was the class boring for you?"

"It's always the same stuff. Nurse Hwang began by saying, '*Having a positive mental attitude is healthy for the mind. Ask yourself what you can do instead of what you can't do.*' Blah, blah, blah… She seems to think that what we think or feel is totally our choice. Is it true, Dr. Yoon? Can you say, '*I'm happy*', when you're miserable? Can you say, '*I can do anything*', when you can't even lift a finger? If I could change everything by my will, I wouldn't be here, Dr. Yoon. I would be a concert pianist, going to every great place in the world—New York, Chicago, Paris, Berlin—you name it, I'd have been there. Accepting one's situation is a wise thing, in my opinion. That said, I'm sick, I can't walk, I'm miserable."

"I see what you're saying, Miss Hyon," Dr. Yoon said. "What Nurse Hwang meant to say is that you have a choice. You can dwell on your unhealthy thoughts and feel miserable all day, or you can say, 'I'm not feeling as bad as two days ago. I'm getting better!' Or you can say, 'I want to enjoy the sunlight rather than worry about rain that might not happen tomorrow.' Does that make sense?"

Hyon said, "When I have pain, that's all I can dwell on, so help me God. But once in a while, I notice the bright sunshine outside my window or see birds chirping and flying around, distracting me from my agony. That's why I like to sit by the window and enjoy as much as I can."

"Good for you! Yes, nature helps us feel better. For instance, when you see a beautiful tree swaying in the mild breeze, you feel free as they are; when you hear birds singing and trilling from your window, you want to imitate them. That's why many poets and writers wrote about nature."

"I wish I could read poems again. My eyes are foggy, as if looking through a glass of milk."

Dr. Yoon abruptly changed the subject. "I'm going to ask you to remember a few things you don't want to remember, alright, Miss Hyon?"

"Ask me, Doctor."

"Do you recall telling me about your son you gave up when he was four years old?"

The woman's expression turned rigid. "Of course I do, Doctor. I've talked about him many times with you. Why do you ask?"

"You will soon find out why. Have you had another dream about him lately?"

"I did, in fact, yesterday. He was still a little boy but was taller and bigger than I remembered. He was talking like an adult, Dr. Yoon. He wore a blue suit and a red necktie and said to me, 'Omma, I've been thinking of you every day.' He acted so grown up, Dr. Yoon! I told my little prince I thought about him every day since he left me when he was four. Do you remember I called him my little prince, because I knew he'd be adopted and didn't want to give him a name he'd lose soon? Anyway, I went on saying that he was such a good boy and how happy I was to see him. Then, a strange thing happened; he turned into a large bird and flew up and was circling over my head, faster and faster. I got scared..." Hyon choked up, making a squeaky noise through her throat and acting as if she'd faint. Dr. Yoon rose, and reaching her oxygen tank, she turned the knob to one side. Hyon breathed normally again.

"You were talking about your dream, Miss Hyon," Dr. Yoon refreshed her memory as she returned to her seat.

"Yes, I was panicky when he turned into a large bird and circled over my head. I was afraid that he would fly out of an opened window, but I couldn't get up from my wheelchair to close the window or catch him with my own hands. Then, I woke up and my little prince wasn't there anymore. Why did I dream such a weird dream, Dr. Yoon?" She grabbed an end of her dress skirt and blew her nose into it.

Michael suddenly burst into tears, surprising everyone in the room. The woman stopped blowing her nose and turned her head in his direction and asked, "Dr. Yoon, who's here besides you and me? I thought we were alone."

"Mother, I'm here!" Michael said as he rose from the chair and rushed to her. Embracing the woman tightly, he sobbed, his shoulders heaving. The room was filled with his sobs.

Dr. Yoon called, "Mr. Hamil, please..."

"*Mother…*?" Hyon said meekly. "Dr. Yoon, who is this man calling me 'mother?' I'm confused. Please tell me…" Then she too broke into tears.

Father Patrick rose. "Min-sook, do you remember me? I'm Father Patrick Anderson. You were in my philosophy class in Sonam College 30 years ago. It was such a turbulent time… Remember?"

"*Father Patrick?*" she asked, looking at Dr. Yoon, her eyes wide. "Dr. Yoon, Father Patrick went back to America after he got into a fight with the policemen beating us students at a demonstration… It was a terrible day… Many students were arrested for demonstrating that day."

"That was me, Min-sook. You have a good memory. I was sent back to Milwaukee, where I grew up and was ordained, and lived there for two decades until I came back to Seoul ten years ago. The man who's holding you now is your son, Michael Hamil!"

"My son?" she asked feebly.

"Yes! There's nothing to be confused about. It's a miracle of *life.*"

Dr. Yoon muttered, "I can't believe this," shaking her head.

Mother and son were both crying now and talking at the same time, oblivious of what Dr. Yoon was saying.

"I knew I'd meet you someday, Little Prince… My prayer is answered."

Michael responded, "Mother, I've lived for this moment all my life. I'm not going to let you go now! I'm going to take you with me if Dr. Yoon will let me. You and I have much catching up to do!"

"I want to be with you more than anywhere in the world, Son. Tell the doctor that I'm going with you."

"Dr. Yoon," Michael said in a congested voice, "please let me take her with me, just for one day. I'll bring her back tomorrow, I promise."

"Where will you take her, Mr. Hamil?" Yoon asked in a controlled voice.

"My apartment in Shinchon. She can have my bed and I'll sleep on the sofa, the two of us alone in my room! We can talk all night and all the next day."

"We can't let you do that, Mr. Hamil. Without her medicine and all the treatments she gets here, your mother cannot survive even one single day."

"Mother, did you hear what Dr. Yoon said?"

"Dr. Yoon," Hyon said in a piercing voice, "I'd rather die today outside these walls than live here a long time, swallowing pills and being stabbed with a needle a dozen times a day! And I'm tired of listening to the screams of dying people, too. Please, let me go with my son, I beg you!"

Dr. Yoon pushed a button under her desk, setting an alarm off. Two men in white gowns rushed into the room without a knock. "What seems to be the problem, Doctor?" one of them asked.

"This meeting is over," Yoon said coldly. "Please take Miss Hyon to her room."

* * *

In the car, returning to Sochun that late afternoon, Father Patrick noticed that Michael was sullen and distant, which didn't surprise him. He was biting his lips like a child fighting back tears after a scolding. Though he had comforted many people, Father Patrick had no words to comfort Michael. He understood Michael's feelings about seeing his mother in such a condition in a place where only dying people lived. It brought his memory of seeing his own mother after returning from Korea in the autumn of 1972. The two of them had a tearful reunion like that of Michael and his mother's. His father had died when he was a teenager, forcing him to search for something greater, something permanent, eventually leading him to choose a life of a priest. His mother had been devastated about his decision; she had dreamt of seeing him happily married and giving her grandkids, like his two sisters. But seeing him returning back to Milwaukee after seven years, his mother had been elated, not understanding that her only son had been deported by the Korean court-order for 'participating in anti-government activities'.

He was glad that he had visited her regularly until she passed away at age 86 in her own home a few years earlier, the

78

home where she had been happy as a wife and a mother of her three children.

"It was quite a day for you, Michael, wasn't it?" Father Patrick broke the silence.

Michael said nothing.

"I'm not sure if you heard Dr. Yoon saying that you could come see your mother as many times as you want but she can't let you take her."

Michael said in a low voice, "Does she expect my mother to live a long time with the deadly chemicals in her system that reduced her to merely bones and skin, unable to walk?"

"No one knows how long your mother can live."

"Does Dr. Yoon know she's dying? Is there any hope that the victims of toxic chemicals can get better with time? You saw her, Father Patrick; she seemed in a lot of pain, besides looking pale and that her head is bald. What's the point of prolonging her life when there is no cure for her?"

"So what are you suggesting, Michael? Let's say that you took your mother to your apartment; how long do you think a woman depending on oxygen tank and her wheelchair can live without them? Can you fix her oxygen tank when she has trouble breathing, like Dr. Yoon did earlier?"

Michael didn't utter a sound.

"And is your apartment wheelchair-accessible? What if she falls and hurt herself? Calling an ambulance is easy, but it can take a long time to show up, depending on the time of day it is and where you're calling from. And it's expensive too! Can you handle the medical bills?"

Michael still said nothing.

"I understand why you want to take her to your apartment, but for her safety, she should remain where she is."

Still no word from Michael.

The sky was now dark, but the highway was two endless streams of bright lights, one stream heading east and the other heading west. Father Patrick thought Michael might have fallen asleep, then he spoke. "I want to give my mother something to remember before she dies. About this time of the year, the scenery along the Han River is breathtaking, particularly at sunrise or sunset. I went there recently, and I thought to myself, if I ever find Mother, I'll bring her there and the two of us would go for a boat ride. The water looks like liquid gold against the bright sunlight, and we'll see groups of birds like snow cranes from the DMZ migrating to the Southern Pacific. You know that the strip of land along the 38th Parallel called 'No Man's Land' was turned into a wildlife sanctuary since the war ended in the 50s, don't you, Father? My mother would love to see those long-necked creatures. When she gets very tired, I'll sing the song she sang to me when she put me to bed—the lullabies, some Korean some German. You told me she was an accomplished pianist when she was in your class. Why does she have to rot away in that hospital like a sick bird dying in a metal cage?"

Father Patrick said, "You sound like you're plotting the murder of your dying mother."

"I'm not."

"Michael, let me remind you that one of the Ten Commandments reads, 'Thou shall not kill'."

"My mother is dying!" he said, in an angry voice. "The Ten Commandments are for the living, Father. In a short time, she'll perish in that hospital. I want her to be free from her suffering. Is that a crime?"

This time, Father Patrick couldn't find words.

That night, Father Patrick could not sleep. *What if Michael actually does something he'll regret for the rest of his life? What he said made sense—'Why not give my dying mother some joy before she dies?' However, what if his mother dies in his apartment? The court will find him guilty of kidnapping or even fabricate the story that he kidnapped her to murder her cold-heartedly for having abandoned him as a toddler. Once caught, his life is in the hands of prosecutors. He'll be incarcerated for a lifetime, if not sentenced to death. Lord, help him!*

Chapter Ten
Kidnapping His Mother

The next day, Father Patrick couldn't be calm after he offered his daily seven o'clock morning Mass. Whenever his desk phone rang, he jumped, but each time he was relieved when the caller asked him for his normal duties—to baptize a baby on the following Sunday or an elderly father in a nursing home was dying and needed an Extreme Unction.

That night, long past midnight, a phone call woke Father Patrick. Dr. Yoon's voice resonated in his ear, nailing each word. "Father Patrick, Maria Hyon is missing from her room."

"I don't understand; why are you telling me that, Dr. Yoon?" he asked, agitated. "She is your patient. And I'm not a detective."

"I'm calling you because I believe Michael might have something to do with her disappearance. According to her nurse, three men dressed like medics came into the room Miss Hyon shares with others and took her on a stretcher. They showed a Request for Patient Transfer order from Saint Mary's Hospital, the nurse said. She called security but they couldn't stop them, because one of them showed a doctor's authorization for her transfer. The only person I can think of is Michael Hamil, because he said he wanted to take his mother with him the day he was here with you."

"Dr. Yoon, I don't believe Michael has the ability to mobilize medics to smuggle his mother out of a hospital. Has a similar incident ever happened there before?"

"Not here, Father Patrick. Usually kidnap victims are men of wealth or politicians or women in marriage disputes, never elderly women as sick as Miss Hyon."

"It doesn't make a sense at all, Dr. Yoon. Michael doesn't have a vehicle to transport a very sick lady. His car is a small passenger vehicle with two doors. He couldn't have attempted to get his mother out of the hospital in it."

"The vehicle they used was a black van and it turned out to have a fake license plate, the security officer told me. He reported it to the police and they're looking for the van in question. Who else could have engineered such a crime except the patient's son, who said, in front of me, that he'd take her out of there?"

"What more can I say but repeat that Michael couldn't have done it?"

"Let me ask you a question, then: how long have you known Michael?"

"About two weeks."

"Not very long then. You introduced him as a 'friend'."

This angered him. "Is there a strict rule on how long you have to know someone before you call them your friend? I knew his father… And Michael is quite a talented musician…" He felt that his argument wasn't strong enough.

"Crimes are committed by all sorts of men, Father Patrick, not only by notorious gangsters. I'd appreciate it very much if you give me a call as soon as you hear from Michael. I also gave the police your name as the one who introduced Michael to me two days earlier."

The phone clicked off. He immediately dialed Michael's number, his heart was racing, but instead of Michael's familiar 'Hello,' a recorded woman's voice said that the number he dialed wasn't a working number.

A week later, he found a letter without the sender's name or address in his mailbox.

Dear Father Patrick,

Probably you're informed of Mother missing from the Rehab Hospital and worried about me and Mother.

We're fine. You were right about Dr. Kim, your former student. After I parted with you that night at your church, after our meeting with my mother and her doctor at the hospital, I called Dr. Kim for help. He and I met at a bar and we talked the next day. To make a long story short, he came with his friend, a Vietnam War veteran named 'Kang,' to pick me up in a large van that had 'Medical

82

Emergency' printed on the sides. It was loaded with dirty hospital gowns and towels, wheelchairs, and a stretcher too. We drove to the Rehab Hospital and parked in front of the 'Drop-Off Patient' sign at the curb. Then we changed into white doctor gowns we found in the van and walked into the building carrying the stretcher. The guard on duty demanded to see our IDs and Dr. Kim spoke to him and handed him a paper. He signaled us to go in and we did. No one stopped us.

In the van, when Dr. Kim heard me say that I'd take Mother to my apartment, he called someone on his cell phone and they talked. When the conversation ended, Dr. Kim said that all was arranged.

'What do you mean?' I asked.

He told me about a friend's riverside cabin that was empty during the winter months, which we could use for a while. Dr. Kim was very kind to me, maybe because he read my father's letter that night he came to your place. Something about him made me believe that he had no hard feelings towards my father, which I'm glad about

Dr. Kim comes here to check on my mother daily, carrying his bulging bag, and Mother feels she's in good hands. She's a different woman today, Father. She likes everything I do for her; she even loves the vegetable soup I make for her with some canned vegetables I found in the pantry. This is a dream coming true for both of us, Father Patrick. She's far from danger, and she's happy.

Thank you, Father Patrick. All these 'miracles' were possible because of you. How could I have found Mother without you? How could I have met Dr. Kim without you? How could I have learned of my father without you? I truly believe that God works through men like you! From the bottom of my heart, I say, God bless you!

Michael Dolan

(Please notice my new name, Father – Michael Dolan.)

Father Patrick took the letter to his lips and kissed it. He was relieved that the mother and son were safe in a place Kim had found for them. On the other hand, he was surprised that a well-respected medical doctor like Kim would get involved in such a crime—kidnapping a patient from a hospital with a fake authorization, which he himself might have signed.

But why didn't he call me to let me know he had helped Michael smuggle his mother out of the hospital? He thought about calling him to give a piece of his mind, but that'd only give the police the piece of evidence they might be looking for, in case his phone was bugged in connection with Min-sook's disappearance. He decided that he had no reason to blow his horn at Kim. The long friendship between them too precious to risk.

Part Two

Chapter Eleven
Mother and Son

It was a rough beginning for Michael and his mother. In the middle of the first night, his mother was confused about where she was and why. Michael reassured her that they were finally together, reminding her how they met two days earlier in Dr. Yoon's office. "Remember, Mother, you said to Dr. Yoon that you'd rather die outside the hospital that day than live there for a long time, swallowing pills and being stabbed with a needle a dozen times a day? Well, you're not there anymore. With some help from Father's old students, we came here. Mother, I'll take care of you. We won't be separated again."

"Thanks for rescuing me, Michael," she said meekly. "I remember now." She held him tightly.

"Everything will be fine, Mother. Now, get some sleep."

She obliged, like an obedient child to her father.

The next day, she made efforts to show Michael that she was better. She tried to walk, clutching Michael's arm. She ate the soup Michael made with the rice and canned food he had found in the pantry.

On the third day, she insisted on cooking. "Remember the rice porridge we ate every day when you and I lived in the Buddhist temple?" she asked. "I can still make it if we have rice and salt." When Michael showed her the rice in a ceramic jar, a bag of black beans and a box of canned corn in the pantry, she was happy. "We can survive two months easily with these," she said.

As time went by, Michael missed his band buddies and rehearsals and concerts. He couldn't contact any of them for fear that it might give the police a clue about where to find him—the suspect who kidnapped his sick mother from the hospital. Even if the police were not looking for him and his mother, how could he leave his mother at the cabin alone and go play with the band?

Their weekly concert had been funded by adoption agencies that made fortunes providing Korean orphans to childless couples worldwide, mostly to American parents. Now that Michael had no income, he might have to look for a job. But for now, he had enough money to last at least two months, or until the owner of the cabin wanted them to vacate the premises, which he doubted. Until then, this was their castle.

He helped his mother walk every day, first inside the cabin, his mother clutching onto his arm, or sometimes using the cane that Michael made for her from a tree branch. But as she gained confidence, they ventured outside too. With her free hand, his mother always carried wooden prayer beads strung on a simple cord like those that many Buddhist monks carried with them.

Once, Michael asked what the beads meant to her. "Each of these beads gave me strength," she said. "When I was weak and couldn't go another step, they gave me strength. When I was in grief, thinking of you thousands of miles away, they promised me that I'd see you someday. When I cursed myself for what I'd done to you, they allowed me to remember you, my Little Prince, who gave me so much joy. I could not have survived all those years without these beads."

His mother had vivid memories of the four years they had lived together in the Buddhist temple. "Son, do you remember the temple's bell ringing loudly at early dawn? It was so loud that all 30 children would wake up, crying. We used to plug your ears with balls of cotton, but it never worked."

"I don't remember that, Mother. But, I do remember the black car that showed up in the courtyard one day and took my playmate Mia and drove away. It was after lunch and we were all outside on the playground. Many of us cried, including me. She never returned."

"Really? I must have forgotten it. I can't even recall who Mia was."

"Mia was very small and cried a lot. The nun, who took care of us that day while you and the other nuns were working in the field, beat us with a thin bamboo stick for crying, and Mia was always hit by her."

88

"Tss, tss, tss... I know the nun you're talking about. Most of the nuns had only one child by the monks who lived at another temple over the hill, but that older nun had three kids by the same monk. She felt trapped, no doubt. Women with broken hearts can be cruel to themselves and others."

"I was too young to know that, Mother. But, a few of us were hit almost every day when the same nun watched us. Strangely, when other mothers were around, she never beat us."

"We didn't know that, and you were too small to report what went on there when we worked in the field."

One day, during a walk along the path leading to the Han River, his mother asked, "Son, you never asked me why I moved to the military base in Yongsan District after you left me and ended up in that hospital. Don't you want to know?"

"I'm sure you went there to earn a living."

"That's a part of it."

"What was the main reason then?"

"To find what life was all about."

***

After I saw you leave, in a stranger's arms, I was heart-broken and bitter—bitter about falling in love with your father and causing your birth unexpectedly. I remained in the Buddhist temple for months because I didn't want to lose my precious memory of you and was afraid to leave. Inside those walls, I could still see you and hear your voice calling me. 'Omma, I'm hungry' or 'Look what I made!' pointing at the woodblocks you had stacked up together.

It was the house rule that after the child was adopted and taken away, the mother packed and left. But the superior nun made an exception for me, perhaps because they were shorthanded in the nursery and they knew I was good with children.

But when I learned of your father's death while I was coping with losing you, I felt the world had abandoned me. I guess he still held a part of my heart, even after he had rejected me mercilessly—telling me never to come see him again. As crazy as it seems now, he was my strength after you were torn

89

from me. I thought about him every day! I still loved him, Michael, as foolish as it might sound. But that day, in May, 1975, when I read about his death and how he was discovered in a creek, I crumbled to pieces.

I had no money and no one to hang on to, yet I couldn't stay there. Sound of the bells woke me early one morning; I left the temple without telling anyone. I walked for two hours to the bus station, and from there, I rode the bus to Seoul without paying anything, at the mercy of the driver. In Seoul, I begged for food and money without shame, because society expected Buddhist monks and nuns to beg. I wanted to find a job as a piano teacher, but who would hire me in a Buddhist nun's habit?

After two nights of sleeping on a bench at a park, like a beggar, I had an idea, realizing that it was a Sunday morning. I showed up at a Presbyterian church nearby, hoping to find a western dress. A man in a gray suit saw me and rushed over to shoo me away, but when I told him I wanted to convert to Christianity, he was a different man. He smiled. He talked to a middle-aged woman passingby and she took me to another room with bags of donated clothing and food items piled up on several tables. I walked out of that church in a black dress with a white lace collar, under a black wool coat.

That evening, I showed up at an American officers club, named Gentlemen and Foxes, on a busy street in Yongsan District. When the manager, a young American man, asked, "May I help you?" I told him I was looking for a job as a bar pianist. "Have you ever played any Gershwin music?" he asked.

I said, "No, but I can learn it." He handed me some sheet music with the title 'Rhapsody in Blue'. I sight-read it and he hired me.

That night, my black dress with white lace collar was replaced with a tight, sleeveless, low-necked red dress with a long tail. It was great sitting on the piano bench again and playing Gershwin's 'Rhapsody in Blue' over and over until long past midnight. Though I had not touched piano keyboards for many years, I sounded pretty good, I thought, as good as I used to. Was it because I kept imagining that I was on the keyboard at Sonam College auditorium packed with listeners?

Sometimes, when I was practicing in the empty hall, your father surprised me, suddenly clapping from somewhere I couldn't see or standing behind me, on the stage. Anyway, every time I ended a piece, American officers whistled and shouted 'Bravo!' As time went by, some officers asked me to join their tables after my performance offering a glass of wine or whiskey. Sometimes, I danced with an officer, but with time, I learned that some officers wanted more than just a dance. I can't talk about all that happened there at the bar, but I had a reason to stay there; I felt I wasn't a simple twig that could be blown away by the wind; I felt I was grounded there, because at least some men cared for me. Some American officers reminded me of your father, tall, handsome, and gentle. But one night, while dancing with a young officer, I became dizzy and found myself stepping on my partner's feet. I believe I fainted.

In the military hospital the next day I had a series of tests. The doctor's verdict was unbelievable. I had a cancerous tumor in my stomach that's common to people who were exposed to water contaminated by toxic chemicals the U.S. military dumped in Korea. It was a death sentence for me.

That's how I ended up in that hospital from where you've rescued me that night. I sometimes wonder whether God punished me for my bad behaviours. But now, I don't feel that way, because you found me there and rescued me. I feel I was rewarded for the hardship I went through as a young woman.

Turning, Michael held her tightly in his arms. "Mother, this is my reward too, being with you like this."

"Yes," his mother said. "We're in a dream, Son. I can hear your voice next to my heart and see you, too, though my eyes are cloudy. This is heaven on earth for me. I hope it's for you too."

"Yes, it is! There is nothing else I want."

"Tell me, Michael, do you have a girlfriend?"

"No, I don't."

"Don't tell me you have never been in love with a girl in America where you lived most of your life."

Michael didn't expect such a question from his mother and stammered. "I… I never have."

91

"Michael, why not? You're a handsome young man, with your father's Irish good looks. And a musician too, like me. You could be an actor if you wanted."

Michael quickly made up a story. "Well, come to think of it, I dated a girl in high school. She was pretty, but she wanted to see me more than I wanted. So, after one year, we broke up."

It was a lie, but Michael couldn't tell his mother the truth, that his young foster mother had taken advantage of him when he was 14. Her name was Diana, a mother of two elementary school kids whose husband was a traveling salesman. It was the most humiliating experience he had ever had. At first, he thought Diana reminded him of his mother when she hugged him tightly for doing dishes or taking the trash to the curb on a trash pickup day.

But as time went by and when her husband didn't return home when she expected him, her behavior would turn ugly and psychotic. One such night, she came into his room, while he was doing homework, crying. He asked her what was wrong and she told him that her husband might be having an affair while traveling. Michael didn't know what to say. He wished she'd leave him alone so that he could finish his homework, but instead, she came over to his desk and touched him all over, kissing him too. He pushed her away, but she didn't give up, her hand fumbling inside his pants. He hated her for humiliating him like that. Finally, he got up, knocked her onto the floor, and beat her with all the strength he had. She called 911. He rode the police car that night to Mercy Boys Home in Austin, Texas, a home for troubled teenage boys.

Did I live there a year or two years?

"What's the matter?" his mother asked, noticing his silence.

"Nothing," he said, with a shrug. "I'm sorry, Mother, I don't have a good story to tell you about girls. They didn't like me, and I could care less about them."

Now the river was in front of them. Seeing a wood boat lying on the sand ahead of them, he changed the subject. "Mother, would you like to go for a boat ride?"

"I don't know. I've never been on a boat."

"It's a perfect day for a boat ride. And I think we can borrow that one for a short time."

92

"Wouldn't the owner get upset if we use it without his permission?"

"We'll be back before he finds out that it's missing."

"If you think it's okay for the owner, I'm fine with it."

Leaving his mother where she stood, Michael walked to the boat, dragged it to the water's edge, and turned towards his mother. "Okay, Mother, get in!" He carefully helped her sit on the center bench, sat on the one behind her, and began to row. The water was chilly on his hands at first, but in a few seconds it didn't bother him.

The current carried them west. A flock of large birds flew over them and he pointed for his mother. "Mother, see those birds? They are snow cranes migrating to warmer temperatures in the Pacific."

"Wow," she said, her pale face blooming with a smile. "Snow cranes are known as the Birds of Immortality. That's why their images are embroidered on newlyweds' pillowcases."

"I didn't know that, Mother."

"I'm sure you didn't. Even young people who were born here and lived here all their lives don't know such old customs. How would you have known it?"

Five minutes later, his mother pointed at some rocks protruding five feet tall ahead and said, "Son, there's a hairy creature clinging on the rock, see it? It looks like a dog or a gray fox."

Before Michael saw it, it yelped as if it had heard what his mother had said.

"Wait, it's a dog," she said. "And it's alive! How on earth did it get there?"

"It must be a stray dog that got washed away somehow and that rock caught it," Michael said.

"Can we save it? We can take care of it!"

"No, I won't risk our lives by trying to save the creature from drowning. We don't have lifejackets! And this dingy isn't ours; the owner will be mad if we ram it into that rock and damage it."

"Son, how can we not even try to save that poor dog?" she said. "We must help all living creatures, Lord Buddha said. It will surely die if we do nothing."

"Mother, I don't want to try it! If we hit that rock, this dingy will split in half and we'll both die!"

She didn't seem to hear him. "How can you be so heartless?" she said accusingly. "If you get a little closer, I can grab it."

The water was white with foam as the current pushed the dingy towards the rocks. "A little closer," his mother ordered, her arms stretched towards the rock, making the vessel tilt to that side.

Panicking, Michael shouted, "Mother, don't move! Please!"

But it was too late. She had leaned towards the rock and the boat slipped from under her. She landed in the water with a loud splash.

With all his might, Michael reached for her, in vain. With the current pushing, the boat flipped and he too landed in water. For a brief moment, his eyes met those of his mother's but the force of the churning water blinded them both. He heard his mother crying, "Son, help meeeee!" He frantically swam towards her, but he just churned more foam without getting closer to her, and his hands scrapped against the sharp edges of the rocks around him. Silence followed, except for the sloshing sounds of water hitting the rocks.

We're dying, he thought. Water kept splashing in his face, forcing him to swallow. He couldn't breathe. As he fought to stay above the water, something touched his hand. He tried to grab it, but it slipped away. Then, he felt it again, and this time he seized a piece of driftwood the size of a fire log floating before him. He grabbed it, and while clinging to it, he looked for his mother, but she was nowhere to be found. Tears filled his eyes and he cried, "Mother, where are you?"

Instead of his mother's voice, he heard water splashing powerfully against the tall rocks, mixed with the whistle of the wind passing. The fear of death numbed him and he managed to tear himself away from the merciless rocks and swam toward the sand beach where they had found the boat. When his feet touched the river's bottom, he waded out of the water. He sat on the sand and cried. 'Mr. Hamil, didn't I tell you your mother could not survive a single day without these walls...' Dr. Yoon's voice rang in his ears. He shouted, as if she stood before him, "But she survived nine days! She didn't want to

94

live in that prison where she was destined to die! I gave her nine days of happiness and freedom!"

Michael jolted when he heard footsteps behind him and the panting of a dog. Turning, he saw a tall man wearing a black wind jacket, khaki pants, a matching backpack slung on one side of his broad shoulders, walking a leashed dog the size of Lassie he'd seen on TV in Texas. *A hiker?* The dog began to bark and the man shushed him, saying, "Calm down, Toby! And be quiet." The dog ignored his owner's command, barking harder and jumping up and down, as if to free itself from the leash. But the hiker pulled it back. Soon, the man and the dog stood before Michael, still shivering, and crying, in soaking wet shirt and pants.

"What happened?" the hiker asked, lowering himself. "Were you swimming in this weather?"

Michael shook his head, unable to stop himself from crying. "We were on a boat… And it overturned near those tall rocks…" He pointed.

"You said we. Who were you with, sir?"

He almost said, 'with my mother', but he caught himself. If he told the truth, that his mother had died while they were boating, this man would surely call the police. Then what? The police would arrest him and eventually charge him with smuggling out a cancer patient from her hospital bed and now for drowning her too.

"I've just lost my dog…" Michael lied. "He jumped into the water when he saw a duck swimming by and went under with it. But now I can't find it. It was a big dog and when it jumped off, the dingy tipped over."

"How sorry I am," the hiker said. "Is there anything I can help you with? You must be freezing…" He swung his backpack from his shoulder, and set it on the sand, took off his wind jacket, and handed it to Michael. "Here, put it on. If I were you, I'd take that soaking sweatshirt off before I put this on."

Michael obliged him. "You're most kind, sir," he said.

The hiker said. "If you can walk to the parking lot down the trail, I'll give you a lift wherever you want to go."

Walking to the cabin would be faster than walking to the parking lot with this Good Samaritan, and who could guarantee that the police wouldn't be waiting for him in the parking lot?

"Thank you, but if you have a phone, I'd like to borrow it to let my friend know where I am."

"Certainly." The man handed him his cell phone.

Michael called Dr. Kim's office, but his secretary answered, so he told her, "Please tell Dr. Kim I need help as soon as possible. He knows where I am. Please tell him I'll be waiting for him."

Loud banging on the door woke Michael. He found himself on the sofa in the front room of the cabin. He must have walked here and fallen asleep as soon as he entered. He looked at the wall clock; it was 12:35 PM. For a moment, he was disoriented and thought, *Mother needs to eat.*

"Michael, it's me, Dr. Kim," the voice said outside the door. Then all was clear. His mother had drowned during the boat ride and Dr. Kim came in response to his call. It felt like a dream—being on the dingy, approaching the hairy creature limply hanging onto the rock, and his mother slipping into the churning water.

"Michael!" the voice called again, with more knocking. He rose from the sofa, rushed to the door, and opened it. Bright sunlight blinded him. In the hazy blur, he made out a man's form standing before him.

"I got your message," Dr. Kim said. "Are you alright?"

"I'm not all right, Dr. Kim."

"What happened?"

"My mother… She drowned."

"She what?"

Michael burst out crying. "It was a crazy idea to be on a boat," he mumbled. "It was my fault!"

Kim entered and forced Michael to turn around and walk to the gray sofa and sit. "Now, tell me what happened," he said as he sat on the other sofa facing Michael.

Tears pouring down his face, Michael told him everything, from finding the small boat left on the sand that morning to the end, where he last saw her. "I told Mother it was too dangerous to rescue the animal, but she said I was being cruel. It happened

96

so quickly when we got close to the rock. The water was rough… And as she reached to grab the animal, the boat tilted, throwing her into the foaming water. I killed her; we should not have gotten in that boat in the first place! I should have died with her."

"I'm sorry, Michael! I think we should call the police to tell them that your mother has drowned. If not, you and I could both end up in jail."

"Can I first talk to Father Patrick?"

"Of course!" Kim dialed and gave him the receiver.

"Father, this is Michael!"

"Michael, so good to hear from you! How is your mother?"

Crying, he gave the receiver back to Kim. "Please tell him what I've told you. I can't talk to him!"

Kim took the phone. "Father, will you be able to come here as soon as you can? Something horrible happened." He then gave him the directions.

Chapter Twelve
A Bleeding Heart

Something horrible happened.

Father Patrick touched his forehead after he hung up the phone. *Lord, be merciful… Min-sook has gone through so much…* He had known all along that Min-sook would die without treatment, and it had happened.

Dr. Yoon had said so. Every day since he received Michael's letter about smuggling his mother out of the hospital with the help of Kim and Kim's friend Kang, Father Patrick had dreaded receiving that call. He even imagined that Michael would say, 'Father, Mother didn't wake up this morning' or 'She fell down and is unconscious'. But instead of Michael, the words, 'something horrible happened' were pronounced by Kim.

Min-sook's pale face with sunken eyes appeared in his mind's eye. "Father," she said in a clear voice, "you once said that God lives in each of us and speaks to us every day, but it wasn't true. Often, a devil tempted me and left me with bitterness about life. Now, God tells me that I'm free, no longer a slave to pain, confusion, and anger. But why am I not happy as a free, carefree person? I asked Him when my salvation would come, but He's silent. Would you please talk to Him? I know He'll listen to you!"

"You're in my prayer, Min-sook. Give Him some time."

"And please tell Michael not to grieve so much. I'm with him, as I have been for the last ten days, but he doesn't know it. He keeps crying. It breaks my heart."

"There's nothing I can do about that, Min-sook. Grieving for the loss of one's loved one is human nature. It's a beautiful feeling, by the way. Let him grieve to his heart's content!"

"Poor Michael…" she said. "Father, please go see him. He's waiting for you."

He rose and gathered his leather pouch, which contained two small bottles—one with holy water and the other with holy oil, just in case. He headed for the door.

His secretary Mrs. Hahn, a widow in her mid-40s, said, "Father, are you coming back for your 3 o'clock appointment?"

"What's the appointment for?"

"Don't you remember the engaged couple? Their wedding is next month."

"That has to wait. Tell them one of my old students has just died."

"I'll tell 'em."

Two hours later, as he followed the arrow sign for Forest Avenue after he exited the highway, looking for house number 1787, he saw Dr. Kim standing before a small wooden structure with red awnings. He veered his old Toyota into the parking lot surrounded by chestnut trees. Seeing Kim's black van, he parked next to it.

Kim rushed to him. "Thank you for coming, Father."

"Is she inside?"

"Father, no," Kim said, making a sad expression. "I should have told you, but I couldn't in front of Michael. His mother isn't here. She drowned and her body washed away!"

"Lord!"

"It was an accident, Father! In fact, Michael almost drowned too. Michael will tell you more about it. All I know is that they were on a small boat when it tilted and she fell in."

"How is he?" Father Patrick asked.

"Not good." Kim shook his head.

They entered through the half-open front door. In a dim light, Michael lay on the sofa, as if sleeping, his left arm on his forehead.

"Father Patrick is here, Michael," Kim announced.

Michael opened his eyes and stared at the ceiling for two seconds before raising himself to a sitting position. When his eyes met Father Patrick's, he bent his head and sobbed quietly. "I should have listened to Dr. Yoon!" he said, his voice quivering. "If I had, Mother would be still alive in that clinic and I could go see her. I let her die!"

"Don't beat yourself, Michael," Father Patrick said firmly. "From what I heard, it was an accident."

"Yes, it was. But I could have prevented it from happening. The problem was, when she found a half-dead dog clinging onto a rock, she went wild. She wanted to rescue it. I said it was too dangerous, but she leaned towards the rock to grab the creature and the boat tilted, dumping her into the water."

"Where did you get the boat in the first place?"

"It was sitting on the sand. It was my idea to go for a ride. But I never thought she'd drown."

A knock on the door surprised everyone except Dr. Kim. "That's my partner, Yim Yong-min, an attorney and a Vietnam War veteran. I told him to come by if he had time." He walked to the door.

A young, slender man in a gray suit walked in, a black binder under his arm. "Good afternoon, everyone," he said politely, as if he were addressing a crowd in court.

Father Patrick stood up and shook Yim's hand.

Michael didn't move; his eyes red and puffy, he looked as if he were in a funeral home.

As soon as he sat down, Yim said, "From what Youn-gill here told me, the odds are against you, Michael."

"Tell me about it," Michael said in a sinking voice.

"Let me lay out a few things that might happen, so you know what to expect. Let's assume that your mother's remains surface somewhere this evening or tomorrow—the police might find her record as a missing person and come after you, the suspect in a possible kidnap case. As far as I know, a warrant for your arrest has not been issued yet. That means no policemen are looking for you, yet. So, you're not in immediate danger of being arrested. Once the warrant is out there, I advise you not to go anywhere."

"Dr. Kim thought I should surrender and explain that Mother died in a boating accident."

Turning to Kim sitting next to him, Yim asked, "Did you tell him that?"

"I did, for his safety; he can be charged as a murderer and face a life sentence, if not a death penalty. I believe the court will be sympathetic if he turns himself in and tells the truth."

Yim grimaced. "Once he's arrested and locked behind bars, it can easily take years before you stand before a judge. And in Michael's case, I guarantee that he can't prove his innocence. There's no witness to prove that she died in an accident. They'll charge him with kidnapping and murder."

"What's your advice?"

"Run for your life!"

There was an audible pause. Silence lingered, as no one spoke.

"Until you're charged with breaking the law," Yim continued, "you're innocent. The prosecutors have to prove that you committed a crime. What will Michael gain by dragging himself into the judicial system, like a dumb cow walking into the slaughterhouse?"

Father Patrick said, "Then you should run, Michael! What are you waiting for?"

"Run away to where?" Michael blurted, his eyes turning red again. "How can you just get on your feet and run? I'm penniless, for one thing. And the police can capture me anytime, anywhere, with a warrant or without!"

Father Patrick dug his hands into his coat pockets and produced a key from one pocket and a few Korean won from another. "You're welcome to stay at our church, Michael. And here is some money that can provide food for a few days."

"Thank you, Father."

Dr. Kim followed Father Patrick's example: "Here, Michael, I have some cash too." He handed him two greenish bills. "It's not much, but you can buy a train ticket to anywhere you want to go within the country with this."

"I appreciate it."

Yim didn't give him anything. He produced a palm-sized notepad and a pen from his coat pocket and scribbled on the notepad and tore off the sheet. "Here," he said. "The man at this address can help you. He's a Vietnam War vet and a client of mine. Tell him you need a Korean Citizen Card. My hunch is you've been using your passport as your ID. Am I correct?"

"Yes."

"What's the name on your passport?"

"Michael Hamil, with my address in Texas. It's a visitor's passport."

"Change your name and use this cabin address as your residence."

"I want to change my name to Michael Dolan!" Michael looked at Father Patrick, as if asking for his approval, and he nodded. "Good Idea!"

"Obviously," Yim said and smiled. "Your father will be glad to hear that!"

Michael was surprised to hear Yim mentioning his father, but on second thought, Dr. Kim must have told him that the dean had fathered a son born of a student... *But how much does he know about me?*

"What is your friend's name, Mr. Yim?" Michael asked.

"Ho In-suk, but he calls himself Uncle Tiger, *Horang-yi Ajusshi*, in Korean, as a joke. He was born in the Year of the Tiger, but mainly he wants to be known as fearless. He was a great soldier, by the way."

"How much will he charge me for making my Korean Citizen Card?"

"All you have to do is to mention my name," Yim said. "I helped him walk out of prison after two years, instead of serving a lifetime for fatally shooting his commander in Vietnam. It was an accident in the jungle, where the visibility was near zero. After he was released, he has helped many people who got into trouble with the Korean authorities, like he himself had. You'll like him."

"Would it be safe to go there? I thought you said I shouldn't be seen by the police."

"I'm glad you thought of that," he said. "I'll take you there; it'd be safer than going by yourself. And I can introduce you to him too."

"That's very generous of you, Mr. Yim!"

Kim said to Yim, wrinkling his forehead, "That means he'll leave his car here. Is it a good idea, leaving his car here, not far from where his mother was drowned?"

"No, it's not safe," Yim said.

"Maybe I'll cover it with something," Michael said, "branches or a tarp?"

"This area isn't searched daily," Yim said, "but when the body is found, a search team will be assigned and men will comb every inch of the place carefully. In no time, the police

102

will match the deceased person's information with whatever they can find. One of us should drive Michael's car somewhere and hide it."

"Hide my car?" Michael cried. "Where? For how long?"

"We don't know! It's for your safety, buddy. Your car has too much information about you—your driver's license, your address, your birth date, your physical descriptions, including the color of your eyes, height, and weight. Should I go on?"

"Father Patrick," Michael turned to him, "can you keep my car at your church for a while? I will follow you and leave my car there. I don't want them to dump it somewhere for good."

Father Patrick looked at Yim and then Kim. "The car isn't in any immediate danger, since the remains of Min-sook have not been discovered yet. Am I correct on this?"

"Yes," Yim said. "But no one can guarantee that she won't be discovered tonight or tomorrow morning. She'll be lucky if she traveled to the east end of the river, which drains into the sea. Once she hits the sea, no one will find her."

"Please stop it!" Michael suddenly shouted, rising to his feet, heaving. "I've just lost my mother, but you're talking as if she were an animal that got washed away... I've had enough for today!" He ran to the door, opened it, slipped out, and slammed the door behind him with a bang. Within seconds, Father Patrick heard the car start and wheels squeal.

Michael is leaving in a hurry, angry and hurt, Father Patrick thought.

The three men looked at one another, speechless.

"That bastard," Yim muttered. "We were trying to help him!"

"He's in grief," Father Patrick said. "Losing the mother he just met and spent a few days with in a boat accident must be extremely painful!"

"What is he going to do now?" Dr. Kim asked.

"At least he has the address of Ho," Yim said in a calm voice. "If he goes there to get his fake Korean Citizen Card, we'll hear from Ho for sure."

Father Patrick said, "Then why don't we all go home and hope for the best?"

Chapter Thirteen
A Fugitive

At a few minutes past ten that night, Father Patrick was on his knees, his eyes fixed on the wooden crucifix hung on the opposite wall, hands folded on his bed, praying for Michael.

The phone on his nightstand rang.

He picked it up, hoping that it was Michael. It was.

"Father, sorry for calling you so late. Is it too late to come see you?"

"Not at all. Where are you?"

"I'm sitting in my car in front of your church."

"I'm so glad to hear that! Use the key I gave you and come in through the side door. I'll meet you there."

Father Patrick quickly wrapped himself in his navy-blue bathrobe and headed to the door.

Michael stepped in, bringing the cold late-October wind with him.

Father Patrick hugged him. "I was worried about you, Michael. Did you have dinner?"

"No. All I need is to talk to you for a few minutes."

"Fine. Let's talk."

They walked to his office down the corridor. They sat facing one another.

"I'm sorry, Father, for storming out of the cabin this morning. I was rude."

"Don't worry about it. We express the way we feel with our actions."

"I couldn't help it!" He bent his head as if fighting not to cry. His eyes showed fear. "I know Dr. Kim and his attorney friend were trying to help me, but the way they talked about Mother…"

"I understand how you feel, Michael. They didn't mean to sound that way, I'm sure. But they're professionals. Professionals use their knowledge and skills like a carpenter handles his project with his tools. Sometimes, when their minds are fully in charge, they shut off their feelings. Does that make sense?"

"It does, Father. I'm a broken man; I can't think beyond the fact that my mother will never come back to me or that I don't know how to find her. She's lying on the river floor somewhere, like Yim said, but I'm on the run. I can't give her a burial, even if she was found."

Father Patrick let out a sigh, his forehead pinched. "I know exactly how you feel, Michael. What you're dealing with is guilt. But take it easy; the dead are gone but the living have to go on living. That's our solemn duty."

Michael was quiet for a long moment. "Father, do you believe in dreams?" he asked.

"Yes. In fact, I pay much attention to my own dreams. And the Scriptures talk a lot about prophets' dreams; for instance, in the Book of Daniel."

"What does it say in the Book of Daniel?"

"It talks about Daniel's prophetic dreams during his lifetime of about 70 years. In one dream, Daniel saw four great winds in the shape of four giant beasts—a lion with eagles' wings; a bear carrying three ribs between its teeth; a leopard with four heads and four large wings; and the last beast with ten horns on his head. He later understood that those four beasts were four empires that would rule Israel with much cruelty. Why do you ask me if I believe in dreams? Did you have a strange dream that you don't understand?"

"Yes. A couple of nights ago, I saw myself falling from the top of a tall cliff to the ocean below. I was very scared. I was falling and falling, without anything to grab on to. I screamed, but nothing came out of my mouth. I woke up remembering the dream. After a while, I went back to sleep and dreamt that I was at the same place, above the ocean, falling from a great height. Then, I hit the water and descended into the bottomless sea. There was music, Father, something I had never heard before but very beautiful and calming. I don't know how long I was there, five minutes or ten minutes? Someone grabbed my arm and I was startled. He lifted me. He wore a scuba diver's outfit and mask, so I couldn't see his face. He pulled me up and up, and I saw sunlight breaking through millions of bubbles that reminded me of large crystal balloons. I was filled with peace and a sense of joy. And then I woke up."

"That's a very interesting dream, Michael. What did you feel when you woke up?"

"I was happy, although I was still sad about my mother. I felt as though someone greater than me was telling me that I would be saved from all my troubles by someone I'll never meet."

"That's a very good interpretation. Dream experts believe that the dream speaks to the person who dreamt the dream, whether it makes a sense or not."

"Thank you for telling me that. There's something else, Father."

"What?"

"I wish I'd visited my father's grave. Remember, Father Murphy wanted to show me the grave behind the hill the Saturday I met him with you? I should have gone with him that day, instead of telling him I'd go later. At that moment, I felt it was the right thing, telling him I can wait, because I was overwhelmed with being at the college father founded and served as the first dean. But, I wish I had gone with him."

"We can go back there, just the two of us, without bothering Father Murphy. It's been long since I visited your father's grave myself."

"Wouldn't it be too dangerous, Father? What if the security guards notice me?"

"As long as they see us together, I don't think they'll bother us. Of course, there's no guarantee."

"When can we go?"

"We can try early in the morning, before students show up, right after my Morning Mass."

"That'd be great, Father. I need him more now than at any time before."

"You're never alone, Michael. Remember, Jesus promised, *'If you remain in Me and My words remain in you, you may ask for anything, and it will be granted'*?"

"But why do I feel all alone?"

"Do you ask Him to be with you?"

"No…"

"Why don't you ask Him?"

"I might try tonight."

"Good idea. And if you feel up to it, stay here tonight and attend my Mass before we visit your father's grave."

"Thank you, Father!"

Chapter Fourteen
A Fugitive

As Father Patrick opened the newspaper at his breakfast table in the kitchen the next morning, a photo of Michael wearing a sweatshirt jumped out. The caption read: 'Kidnap-Murder Suspect at Large'.

The Shinchon District police are looking for American citizen Michael Hamil in connection with the kidnapping and murder of his mother, Hyon Min-sook, a patient at the U.S. Military Cancer Treatment Center in Yongsan District. Hyon was removed from the hospital on the night of October 6th and drowned in the Han River ten days later, according to the police report. Her almost-unrecognizable remains surfaced last night, about four kilometers east of the dumping station, and were sent to a forensic lab for an autopsy. The suspect is believed to be Hyon's son, half-Korean, half-American, 6 ft. tall, weighs 180 lbs., and speaks both Korean and English fluently. The Yongsan District Police are offering a reward of 10 million won for information leading to the arrest of this kidnap-murder suspect.

Father Patrick put his coffee cup down on the table and headed to his office, carrying the crumpled newspaper. Michael lay on the sofa asleep, breathing heavily, his head resting on one armrest and his feet on the other, his arms crossed, as if he were cold. "Michael, wake up!" Father Patrick said firmly. "I'm sorry to give you bad news, but you can't stay here. The police are looking for you!"

Michael sprang up.

"Read this."

After reading it, he asked, "Does it mean we can't go to my father's grave?"

"Yes."

"What must I do, Father?"

"If the police find you here, you and I both will be in trouble. Have you considered finding the man named Ho, who can make your Korean ID card?"

"Not really, because the Korean immigration office doesn't give any foreigner a citizen card before he or she has lived here five years without violating any laws. That guy is running an illegal operation, for sure. It's puzzling why Mr. Yim thought that Ho could help me."

"I'm glad you ruled out that option. I have to say 7 o'clock Mass, but our cook will bring you breakfast. When I return in about an hour, I'll help you find a safer place to stay for a while."

"Thank you, Father. But where would you hide my car parked outside the church?"

"Behind the woodpile in the back. I'll cover it with a tarpaulin."

"Thank you!"

The church was empty except for a dozen old parishioners. While saying Mass, Father Patrick's mind focused on Michael. *Who would offer their place to hide a crime suspect? And what would the parishioners think of me if they discovered that their pastor was hiding a suspect in church property?* Some church elders hadn't been too fond of their American pastor, who allowed 'girls' to serve him during Sunday Mass and often played baseball with teenage boys on the church lot for everyone to see. But he couldn't kick Michael out of his office until he found a safe refuge for him.

Ending Mass a bit sooner than usual, he rushed to the rectory.

His long-time secretary, Mrs. Hahn, a widow, was waiting for him. "Father, where is your friend?" she asked, her arms crossed.

"He was in my office when I left. Did you serve him breakfast?"

"I tried. But he was gone when I got there. And you know what, Father?"

"What?"

"Your new black suit is missing from your closet, and so is your briefcase that you always keep next to your desk!"

"Are you sure?"

"Why would I lie to you, Father?"

Father Patrick had a mixture of feelings—he was sad and glad. Sad because Michael was gone; glad because the police would not show up at his door, looking for him.

"Father, we should report him to the police."

"That's out of question, Mrs. Hahn."

"Why? He stole your new suit and a leather briefcase full of important documents in it, didn't he?"

This angered him. Turning to her slowly, he said, "Mrs. Hahn, is it necessary to remind you that Michael is my friend whom I invited to stay with me? Whatever he took with him is my business, not yours. I'd appreciate it if you show some respect to my guest."

Bowing quickly, she headed back to the office.

* * *

Michael walked fast towards the bus station, wearing Father Patrick's black priest garb without a Roman collar. He wished that the sleeves were longer and less tight around his shoulders. He found himself pulling the sleeves of the arm that carried the briefcase. He tried to look casual, but he kept turning around to see whether the police were on his tail. His heart palpitated whenever a police car passed him or someone looked at him. The thought that millions of people might have seen his photo and read the article under 'Kidnap-Murder Suspect at Large' made him want to find a hole somewhere and hide. But, where could he find a hole large enough to hide him in this densely populated city of 20 million people?

A place came to mind: the 'ruin' he had passed five years earlier during his 10-day 'Adoptee Home Visit Program' here in Seoul. Charlie and he both had heard their tour guide, a young woman with bright-red lips, describe the ruin as a mysterious and haunting place that attracted younger tourists to Seoul. "Look at that ruin on your left," she had said, pointing. "That building was once a schoolhouse built by an American

110

missionary named 'Zeller', but it was bombed during the war. It was never repaired, because it would cost much more than building a new place, so they built on the south side of the Han River instead. But from historians' point of view, that was a waste. This building produced many of the Christian scholars and educators we know today. The sad part is that today the building serves as hiding nook for communist spies, murderers, and thieves."

Michael vaguely remembered it being a two-story structure whose windows were boarded up with rotten wood panels, had some roof tiles missing, and weeds growing in the gutters. *If the structure served as a hiding place for communist spies, couldn't it hide me for a while?* He also remembered that it was across from the long stonewall bordering the famous Yi Dynasty palace named Gyongbok Palace, the home of the last king of the Yi Dynasty that was abolished by the Japanese when they officially annexed Korea as their colony in 1910. Remembering the money Father Patrick and Dr. Kim had given him the night before, he decided to take a taxi, considering that a hundred or more eyes would stare at him in a bus, while only one pair would in a taxicab.

He was right about choosing a taxicab. The driver never uttered a sound after Michael told him his destination. Ten minutes later, he handed the driver 30,000 won, about 6 American dollars, and walked down the long, crumbly stone staircase leading to a dried creek some 20 yards below. The gravel under his feet crunched, making musical noises as he descended. The skeleton of the two-story building was just the way he had seen it five years earlier. The front steps were covered with tangled vines and drying weeds and the windows were boarded up. The roof had sunken on one side and a few rusted metal sheets lay over that area. Stepping on dried vines and weeds, he reached the front door. Its paint was faded and peeling, so he couldn't tell whether it had once been white or light gray, and the doorknob was severely rusted. Cautiously, he tried the doorknob and it turned. *Is someone living here?*

It was dark inside, because all the windows were covered from the outside. On one side of the room, broken chairs and small tables were piled up, as if the residents had attempted to move them but changed their minds at the last minute. The blackboard on the wall opposite him had some illegible words written on it. The floor squeaked whenever he moved. In the faint light, spider webs hung from the once-white ceiling that was now dark gray, like in a horror movie.

Seeing a wooden staircase in the corner, he decided to explore upstairs. Every step he climbed, the boards under his feet squeaked and the noise echoed through the whole building. At the top of the staircase, he let out a sigh of relief. There seemed to be two wings on this floor, each with several rooms on both sides, each room with a dozen wooden bunkbeds that were missing springs and mattresses. Posters hung on each wall. One read, 'Own your future! Every moment counts'; another read, 'Diligence is the key to your future'; still another read, 'Time shouldn't be wasted: Make *time* work for you'. He figured that the building had been a boarding school before it was closed and abandoned.

In the last room, smaller than all others he had looked in, he decided to rest. He sat on the floor, his back against one wall. He was relieved to know that he could hide here for a few days. But then he had no food to survive on. *Why didn't you buy some non-perishable food from the street vendor?* He scolded himself. *I had no time! I had to run for my life wearing Father Patrick's priest garb, didn't I?*

He was hungry and tired. His legs stretched, and with head against one wall, he soon heard himself snoring.

He's on the stage of the New Age Theater, playing with his band. Charlie's band piece *The Promised Land in the Far East* was approaching climax, with loud drum rolls and everyone singing at their top of their voices, "*We've come a long way, friends; and we'll walk together, thick and thin; 'til we find our promised land in the Far East.*"

Something woke him, a sound or a voice. Startled, he opened his eyes.

A bright light shined in his eyes. *Where am I, on the stage?* His left forearm automatically went up to shield his eyes, but from under his arm he saw a pair of mud-smeared boots planted before him. He remembered where he was now. *The vacant building by the old palace.* He remembered walking out of Sochun Catholic Church too, wearing Father Patrick's black

112

suit whose sleeves were too short for him. *Sorry, Father Patrick!*

"Are you our new member?" a man's voice asked.

"*Your new member?* No. I… I just got here a while ago. I thought this place was deserted."

"We use this place for a meeting every once in a while," the same voice said. It was an unfriendly, square sort of voice. "If you tell me why you're here, I'll tell you my story too. Whatever we exchange between us tonight must remain between us, for safety's sake, agreed?"

For safety's sake? The words comforted Michael. On second thought, he knew better than to believe a total stranger's words. How many times had he been tricked by men? Bob and Jimmy, the drug dealers and fake artists in Texas, the first perpetrators he and Max had encountered in their teens. And the guards at Mercy Boys Home in Austin! Once they tricked the boys by saying that many guards were sent for training on such a day, hinting that they could try to run away. But when some boys, including Michael, actually tried to escape through a hole under the wire-fence at night, a dozen guards rushed to them, each with a flash light and wooden bat, and captured them like merciless hunters capturing wild boars.

"Would you please turn that light off?" Michael asked. "I can't see anything!"

The light flicked off with a 'click' and suddenly everything was inky black, as if the end of the world had come without notice. It took a few seconds for his eyes to make out the vague contour of a man standing before him like an onyx statue. This man was at least a head shorter than Michael himself but was sturdily built, with broad shoulders.

"Thank you," Michael said. "I'm homeless, as you can see. I'm looking for a job so that I can find a place to stay and feed myself. It's a long story…"

"Would you like to know about a money-making opportunity?" the man asked.

"Yes, please!"

"Did you read in the papers that the police are looking for a man who kidnapped his mother from some cancer clinic and drowned her? A manhunt is going on along the river at this

113

very moment with the reward of 10 million *won!* Not bad money for a man like you."

"'*A man like me?*' What about you?" Michael asked tartly. "Don't you want to make money?"

In the dark, Michael saw him coming closer and sitting beside him on the floor, only two feet away from him.

"Brother," the man said, "I'm not homeless like you. In fact, I consider myself a fisherman, like the Bible talks about a fisherman who catches souls that swim in the wrong body of water. I cannot go after a fugitive to gain money. Actually, I was sarcastic about a money-making opportunity. I'm sorry."

This was totally unexpected. "You sound like a preacher."

"In fact, I am," he said in a non-negotiable manner. "I'm the leader of a small group of men called 'The Good News Deliverers'. The men in my group were once judged as criminals and sentenced to serve years in prison but are now lifted by the one who created the universe. Recently, prison officials, influenced by many Christian ministers' suggestions, changed the rules and made some exceptions. In short, the prison inmates, with some exceptions, can choose to do *right* for the *wrong* they did in the past by participating in the government programs helping North Koreans. Our group delivers North Korean Christians their living water—Bibles. It is a divine plan. Remember what Jesus said in John 3:15? He said: '*Unless one is born of Water and the Spirit, he cannot enter the kingdom of God… You must be born again.*' My men are born-again Christians."

Michael didn't know what to think. He had not anticipated hearing Bible passages in such a place and time. He hadn't even been in the church where Father Patrick preached on Sundays in the town of Sochun. What irony was this? "Tell me more, sir," Michael said.

"Gladly, brother."

Brother…? Me?

"I've been in and out of North Korea for nearly ten years to collect data about its military, its nuclear program, its starving people, but on the side I've been involved in delivering Bibles to a small group of North Korean Christians with our friends in Dandong, China. Dandong shares the border with North Korea, and my friends have contacts with the North Korean Christians.

114

I've been arrested by the North Korean patrolmen several times at the border but miraculously I managed to escape each time and continue what I strongly believe in—delivering Bibles to those who are in need. North Koreans are starving not only for food but for the good news of the Gospels too. I consider them plants deprived of sunlight and water. That's why our group has been meeting here, at least twice a month."

"Do you mind if I stayed while you meet?"

"Of course not. I don't own this place, if that makes you feel better. Let me tell you something else about what we do: the world seems to believe that North Korea has been a godless country since communism took over at the end of WWII, but it isn't true. During 36 years of Japanese occupation of Korea, which ended on August, 1945, most of the churches, Christian schools, monasteries, and convents operated by Western missionaries were in North Korea, only a few in the South. That said, Japanese in Korea did not persecute Christian ministers; if they didn't love them, they tolerated them. That's why all those churches and Christian schools survived. But that changed after the Russian Army moved into northern Korea on August 12, 1945, at the request of Kim Ill Sung, Kim Jong-il's father. This happened three days after Japan turned into a melting pot when the U.S. pilots dropped atomic bombs in Hiroshima and Nagasaki in early August in 1945. Kim Il-sung's purpose for leading Russian soldiers to his homeland, of course, was to disarm Japanese occupation forces in Korea but he saw a great chance to rule the entire country, united and whole. You know Kim Il-sung fought against the Japanese as a guerrilla leader for many years, don't you?"

"No, I'm not familiar with Korea's history at all."

"It was a crucial time in Korea after WWII ended with Japan's unconditional surrender to the Allies. Anyway, in response to USSR's blatant move to the Korean peninsula, the U.S. sent two divisions of occupation forces in Japan to southern Korea a month later, on September 12th, 1945. This unexpected change caused Western missionaries in the North to escape to the South but some vanished without leaving a trace. After North Korean communists invaded South Korea five years later, in June, 1950, they rounded up about 10,000 so-called intellectuals—scientists, engineers, professors, and religious leaders, including several hundred Western missionaries and the prisoners of war—and forced them into a death march, crossing a distance of about 110 miles on icy mountainous terrain to prison camps along the Yalu River.

"Today, South Korea has nearly 5 million Christians out of 45 million total population, but no one knows how many Christians are in the North. What our group is doing is helping God, by reaching out to His forsaken people in the North."

Michael felt safe. He could trust this man who was claiming that he and his group were doing God's work for Christians in North Korea. "I didn't mean to hide anything, brother, but I didn't tell you that I'm that man you told me about, the kidnap and murder suspect the police is…"

The man raised his hand towards Michael. "Please, I'm not here to hear your confession, brother. Every man in my group has a similar story to tell, but the rule is we don't talk about the past nor do we judge each other's wrongdoings. And further, we each accept one another as we are and follow Jesus' footsteps together. Only those who understand what our Lord Jesus went through on earth understand His death, resurrection, and holiness, too. Does that make sense?"

"Yes."

"Then let me ask you this! Would you like to work with us?"

Chapter Fifteen
Miracle Man

In the next hour, Michael learned much about this 52-year-old Presbyterian minister, Reverend Min Kyu-sok, who had invited him to work with his group. After graduating from Saint Paul Presbyterian Seminary here in Seoul, Min said, he worked at a small church named the Church of Shepherd as an assistant pastor for a few years. "That church still exists," he said.

One early morning, Min woke up dizzy, confused, with one side of his body not responding to normal commands. His voice was gone too. Realizing something was wrong, he crawled out of his sleeping mat, crawled to the door, and alerted the housekeeper downstairs by kicking the door of his bedroom. Later, in the emergency room, he learned in dismay that he'd had a stroke that blocked a blood vessel supplying blood to his brain. He was only 30 years old.

"After two weeks of treatment, I was wheeled out of the hospital, still paralyzed on my left side. I felt helpless: I couldn't dress myself, put myself to bed at night, or get up in the morning. Everything I used to do—reading, writing, feeding myself—were impossible tasks for me, unless someone helped me. Unable to do anything, I wished I could die.

"But one night, I had a strange revelation that still seems surreal. I had fallen asleep while praying in my wheelchair, and a bright light woke me. At first I thought an ambulance was outside my window and I was scared, but the light was coming from a man standing before me. I almost lost my mind. 'Are you Jesus our Lord?' I asked Him. And He answered, 'I am'. I said, 'Be merciful, Lord, and heal me. How can I do your work as your chosen servant in this condition? I can't go anywhere or do anything without other people's help, and worst of all, I can't talk to those You send to me to guide'.

"'That's why I'm here,' he said in a clear voice. He then handed me a small glass filled with what seemed like red wine. 'Drink this and rise from that chair. You'll be unsteady for a few days, but you can walk. Tell people that you got strength from praying, nothing else. I have a place for you, in North Korea. You'll know when the time comes'.

"Then He vanished. A part of me denied what had just happened but another part believed it. I wasn't imagining; it had happened before my eyes and His voice was still ringing in my head. 'He was here! He was real,' I kept saying, as if proving to myself what I saw and heard actually happened. Unbelievably, I rose to my feet at that very moment and was able to walk, unsteady at first. The following Sunday, the congregation was shocked when they saw me walking to the podium on my two feet. When I said Jesus heard my prayer and healed me, the congregation went wild, crying and shouting, 'Hallelujah! Praise the Lord,' as if the end of the world had come.

"Everything fell in place after that, Michael. I soon met someone who lived in Dandong, China, a town on the Chinese and North Korean border. His baptismal name was Paul. From what I heard from him, North Korean secret agents were cracking down on Christians who were gathering secretly to pray and encourage one another not to lose hope in God. I felt that my service was needed there, in the North.

"During the past ten years, our team has delivered 1,500 volumes of Bibles to North Korea through my friend Paul and his peers in Dandong. And we also helped my Christian brothers and sisters living in that godless country called 'Kim Dynasty' in any way we could—delivering food, clothing, and medications. Paul and I also helped several dozen North Koreans defect to the South, who are now living in *Hanawon*, meaning 'Home for Unity' in Ansong, a town 30 miles east of Seoul."

"It's such an amazing story, Reverend Min!" Michael said.

Min added that the trip Michael would join would be his 23rd. "In my new team we have five men, not including you. They each have a black belt in Taekwondo, swim like a dolphin, and speak like North Koreans, without a Southern accent. Three of the five were officially pardoned from their

118

earlier crimes by the South Korean president and were released, but two others will be released too."

On the second day, in the same room, the first Good News Deliverers' meeting took place in the boarding school. A burning candle in the corner revealed the deterioration of the building—holes in the ceiling, graffiti on the walls, dirty wooden floorboards. The smell of something rotting and dust was strong.

Since they didn't have the luxury of tables and chairs, they all sat on the wooden floor covered by a large bamboo floormat.

"Welcome, everyone," Rev. Min began the meeting. "Our fifth journey this year to North Korea will take place in six weeks, as you are aware. We have a new member, Michael Dolan. He's replacing Mr. Chun whom we lost during our last trip while we swam across Imjin River. Let's pause in silence to pay tribute to our beloved brother Chun."

Each man lowered his head and remained in that posture, praying.

When done, Min said, "Please welcome our new member Michael here, who lived in American most of his life before returning to Korea three years earlier."

The shortest man in the group, one in his mid-30s, looked at Michael and then Min. "Boss, why do we need to tell our new member about the tragic accident that ended the life of our dear friend Chun? Michael might not want to go with us now."

Min said, "It's better to know than not knowing, in my opinion. It only tells him that we're not going to the North on a picnic." Turning to Michael, he said, "It's a dangerous trip, Michael. Do you still want to go with us?"

"Absolutely," Michael said.

"Why don't you tell us about yourself, not what you've shared with me the other day but what you can do for the people in the North? In other words, spell out what talents you have and why you joined us."

Michael spoke with ease and confidence. "I've been a singer and a guitarist for 3 years after I returned to Korea, having lived in the U.S. more than 20 years. If I'm allowed to bring my guitar along, I'll entertain you with the songs I know."

"Wonderful," Min said, and all others nodded in agreement. "Please play for us every night if you like, Michael. Music brings us close to God. I am glad that you're with us!"

Michael said, "For the North Korean Christians, I can promise my very best in delivering the Bibles. As a teenager living in Texas, I delivered something to a man, not knowing that it was an illegal substance and was caught by the police. But this time, it's the good news of our Creator. I'll be very careful not to get caught."

"And you'll be caught too!" Rev. Min said. "When that happens, the secret police will torture you to get information about your accomplices. What will you do then?"

"I'll never say a word about any of you, trusting that you'll do the same."

"Very good. The safety of our team depends on each one of us. The rules of the game are keep your mouth shut and don't stick your nose in others' business! Make sense?"

"Yes, Boss."

Turning to a slim and fairly handsome man about Michael's age, Min said, "Dong-il, introduce yourself to Michael."

He seemed nervous. "Mmm… me, Boss?"

"Yes, you!"

"I… I'm a whistle blower. I… I lead the way and signal when I see danger ahead."

The older man next to him volunteered. "I'm a former army sergeant who turned to needle business after I was released from the military prison where I was for punishing a private too severely. As my sign of remorse for what I've done, I treat people with the ancient Chinese art of acupuncture. If anyone of you gets sick during our mission, I'll fix you. Call me 'Needle Doctor'."

The third man, with thinning hair and crooked nose, introduced himself as Boxer. "Once I was a notable boxing champion, but my punching technique got me in a serious trouble after I caught a burglar. My punch killed him and sent me to prison. I promise I'll only use my fists when our lives are threatened."

The last man, the man in his early 60s with a graying moustache who sat next to Michael, called himself 'Coach'. He briefed that he was in charge of training and said, "Please don't make me yell at you. Do as I expect you to as gentlemen. Then we can be good friends."

Min said, "Coach, would you tell us what we'll do the next few days before we hit the road? Our new member here," Min tilted his head towards Michael sitting next to him, "will appreciate it."

"My pleasure, Reverend Min," the coach said. Turning to Michael, he said, "I'll wake you up before sunrise, and after a quick breakfast, we'll walk ten kilometers to the top of that hill," he pointed over this shoulder. "In the pond, we'll swim. The water is freezing cold by this time of the year, but you'll get used to it. You have to, because we'll have to cross rivers on the way North and coming back too. In the afternoon, we'll do Taekwondo and other martial arts for physical strength and mental alertness. As the reverend said, the jobs waiting for us aren't a piece of rice cake. They're tough!" He stopped and looked at each man. When no one said anything, he said, "By following my instructions closely, you can reduce the chances of being caught and sent to a labor camp. Understand?"

"Yes, sir!"

Chapter Sixteen
A Man Named Coach

The first thing Michael heard the next morning was a shrill whistle. It was dark, with no hint of sunrise. Each man washed in the bathroom, using a tall bucket of water, and brushed his teeth with salt from a small bowl sitting on a stool next to the bucket. Then, they ate hot rice-cakes, boiled corn, and boiled eggs that the Needle Doctor cooked in a cast-iron pot over an open fire. When the sky turned gray, with clouds turning pink and lavender, they filed out of the boarding school carrying bamboo baskets containing their lunch, towels, and swimming trunks. As they walked, they sang one song after another that Michael didn't recognize, yet he enjoyed listening.

Two hours later, a broad view of a forest and brownish field that had once been a rice paddy or vegetable garden or cornfield opened before them. "Look," Coach said, his hand pointing north. "There is the DMZ at 38th Parallel."

Everyone stopped walking and looked in the direction Coach pointed. "The birds we see over there have their nests in the No Man's Land along the 38th Parallel, which's a strip of land between the two Koreas about 150-mile long and 1.5-mile deep. We can easily see it through binoculars on a clear day. But it's an eternity away in a political sense. If you want to get to the north side of that DMZ, you'll be shot at by South Korean patrolmen."

Arriving at the pond ten minutes later, the group changed into their swimming trunks and jumped into the freezing water. They competed with one another, swimming up and down ten times. In a half hour, they changed back to their street clothes, shivering and chattering their teeth, gathered around the fire the Coach had made, and ate lunch—the leftovers from the breakfast.

"Anything tastes good after a good workout," the Whistle-blower said, smacking his lips, not totally satisfied.

"It's nature," Coach said in an all-knowing manner. "I've never had a bad meal outdoors. And this place is close to heaven."

"Not too close, I hope," Boxer said. "I don't want to go to heaven too soon, if I can help it. After I was relieved from the prison after 15 years with a new mission, I feel I was reborn. I don't want to lose my second chance at any cost."

"Same here," Needle Doctor said. "We're lucky to have a second chance."

The rest of the day, they practiced martial arts in the open field under the broad sun until Coach blew his whistle.

On the way back from training one evening, Coach approached Michael. "I reckon your last name is Dolan."

"Yes, it is!"

"Are you related to an American Jesuit priest by the name of Father John Dolan? He was the dean of Sonam Catholic College in Shichon. You remind me of him."

How does he know my father? Michael thought. Yet he wasn't eager to ask Coach that question. "Dolan is a common Irish name," he said vaguely. "I was born here in Korea but lived in the U.S. for more than 20 years before I returned here."

"Hmmm! Interesting. That American priest hired me shortly after I defected to the South in 1965. It doesn't seem that long ago, but it's been 37 years."

"Defected, Coach? Were you a North Korean?"

"Yes. I was the very first border patrolman in the rank of captain who defected to the South. Before me was a pilot who flew a Russian MiG-15 fighter to Kimpo Airport one morning without a scratch and received a big award from the American government. I made enough buzz too, though no one awarded me for crossing the 38th Parallel, risking my life."

"I've never met a North Korean defector before. How did you feel about leaving North Korea after having lived there many years? Weren't you afraid of dying?"

"I was. But I had been thinking about it long enough that I wasn't that scared. I knew I'd eventually die on my job by stepping on a mine or from starvation or in a labor camp if someone snitched on me. That morning, during our duty, we found one of our colleagues dead on the roadside in a fetal position, a bullet hole in his head. I knew the time had come for me to run away. When no one was looking, I slipped out of my position and ran into a ditch filled with tall weeds by the road and hid in it. I heard shots firing and footsteps approaching, so I got up and ran south. As I crossed the dividing line between the two Koreas, I was hit in the back and fell."

"How did you survive after having been shot? You could have bled to death."

"I could have, but two South Korean guards came within minutes, firing at my comrades who were trying to kill me. They loaded me onto a stretcher, and carried me to their mobile urgent care unit nearby. My injury wasn't serious; a bullet went through my flesh near my left hip-bone, causing me to bleed. Still, I was flown to a large hospital in Seoul for a treatment. Two days later, I was interviewed by a dozen reporters, each carrying a camera. I can't tell you how many times they asked me the same questions over and over: *Why did you runaway? Didn't you know your fellow North Korean guards were going to kill you? Do you feel safe being here, only 35 miles from the border—from the men who shot you?*

"I answered earnestly. When the South Korean CIC (Central Intelligence Corp.) officials heard me say that North Korea had dug long tunnels under the 38th Parallel wide enough for infantry to cross the DMZ within an hour in preparation for another surprise attack against the South, I was suddenly a hero. I appeared on TV and was invited to meet with a large group of professors and experts on global issues and talk about my reasons to escape North Korea. That was where I met the tall American priest I've told you about, Father John Dolan, the dean of that American Catholic college."

Michael was alert. *Was this the man Father Patrick had mentioned, the man whose name appeared on the newspapers as the murder suspect when Father's mysterious death was reported? What was his name…?* Then it came. "Are you Mister Wong, by any chance?" Michael asked.

He stiffened. "Yes, I am. Wong Tae-sup. Who told you about me?"

"Father Patrick Anderson."

124

"Father Patrick!" he shouted. "I heard that he's back in Seoul. He was a young priest with guts, as I remember. He got into a fight with armed police during a student demonstration and was ordered to leave Korea. How do you know him?"

Michael reluctantly told Coach the whole story about how he met Father Patrick at his church in a small town named Sochun, which opened up a path in his life he had not known existed, and revealed himself as Father Dolan's illegitimate son. He didn't say anything about his mother, not knowing where that information would lead.

"You and I are connected through your father," he said, his face lit with a friendly smile. Lowering his voice to a whisper, he said, "Your father surely was a modern-day Abraham, in my opinion."

"I don't know what you mean by that."

"He was a good man. As a good man often makes enemies, there were men who didn't like him, I can tell you that."

"Let me ask you a question, Coach. Father Patrick said that your name was mentioned in an article that reported my father's death. Is that true?"

"How does he know?" he asked in a defensive manner. "He wasn't in Korea at the time; he was in America, in a town called Milwaukee."

"But you were mentioned in the article, were you not?"

"What does it matter? They couldn't find anything about me that linked me to his death. If they did, I'd still be sitting in prison."

"It matters to me that you're mentioned in the papers."

Wong's jaw muscles twitched; he seemed to be collecting his thoughts. "The reason the newspapers mentioned my name was because people at the College saw me leave with your father a day before he was found dead in the creek. In other words, I was the last man your father was with and spoke to."

"Why were you and my father together that day?"

"He asked me to come along on his regular visit to a convent in the northern part of Seoul to say Mass and hear confession. For a few previous days, the situation at the College was worse than ever. Students kept demonstrating as the death toll of Korean troops in Vietnam rose to nearly 5,000. The Special Forces moved into our campus with clubs, rifles, tear gas bombs, water hoses... You name it and they had it. Your father was quite agitated that day, perhaps even fearful about what might happen to him, because he had agreed with President Park to support government policy when he entered the country earlier and felt he was failing in his duty as a missionary and the dean of the school. In other words, he felt he had betrayed his students to keep his promise with the government."

"Where was this? Did you talk with him in the car or in a coffee shop?"

"In the school van he was driving. He said that when the Vietnam War suddenly ended and his surviving students returned, their spirit crushed as the losers of the battle, he felt as lost as they were. He was on the verge of breaking down, the way I saw him. He seemed he couldn't see well enough to know where he was going, the van in and out of its lane. In my unsophisticated words, I told him not to judge himself so harshly and that what he had done here in Korea was grand. 'People will remember you, Dean Dolan,' I said. You know how he responded? 'Mr. Wong, our vulnerability as men brings us all to the same level. It doesn't matter how educated you are or what influence you have in this civilized world. But as the dean of the College, I agreed with the president in sending my students to the war, where almost 5,000 Korean troops had died, including about 182 students from our College. I am responsible for that many lives of my students, to say the least. I deserve punishment'."

"Did he say anything about me?" Michael asked.

"No, he didn't. He was beyond himself."

"Were you aware of his relationship with my mother? What I mean is..."

"I know what you mean, Michael," Coach said. "Yes, I was. In fact, some employees working there had a vague notion that something 'sticky' was happening between the dean and that charming, talented pianist-student. Let me put it this way: Hyon Min-sook was a jewel to your father's eye."

"What do you mean by that?"

Coach cleared his throat before he began, "No one really knew much about your mother, except that she grew up with her aunt's family, having lost her parents as an infant during the war. She often practiced on the grand piano in the auditorium until long after the classes ended and students left for the day. One late evening, I went there to inspect water damage on the back wall behind the stage a co-worker had told me about, and she was there, practicing under the bright stage light. I was careful not to disturb her, not to be polite, but I enjoyed listening. She was a lovely young lady, besides being a promising pianist who shined at every school function. Unexpectedly, Father Dolan came in through the side door next to the parking lot in his gray exercise outfit. He sat in a seat near where he had entered and listened, obviously unaware of me backstage.

"I believe your mother was playing something called *The Moonlight Sonata,* which she had performed before. After a few minutes, when the music got faster and louder while her hands raced up and down the keyboard, he quietly rose and approached the stage. The girl wasn't aware of the intruder and kept on playing. To my dismay, he walked up onto the stage and stood behind her. The music stopped. I saw him seating himself next to her, on the piano bench. They began to play together a song I wasn't familiar with. Until that moment, I hadn't been aware that the dean could play piano. After about five minutes, silence fell in the auditorium.

"In dismay, I saw two images merging into one as the dean gathered her in his arms and sank down to the dark floor under the grand, and I lost sight of them. My imagination ran wild. I had the urge to call security to report what was happening, but I couldn't actually do it. Instead, I made noises by dragging the wooden stool next to me. The dean came up, glanced in my direction, and slipped away into the darkness behind the stage. The girl surfaced too, and seated herself again on the piano bench to button her blouse. Then she too vanished behind the stage wall."

"Did you see them together again, Coach?"

"Never."

"Coach, didn't it bother you that the dean was fooling around with a young Korean female student in the empty auditorium when College was out? You even described him as a 'modern day Abraham Lincoln'. Why?"

Coach threw a sharp glance in his direction. "Michael, let me give you my thoughts about life, okay? Don't judge anyone from the top of your head. Whether you're a priest or a criminal, you have only one chance in life. You can pray all day, every day in a chapel, oblivious of the world outside, or you can accept obstacles, dream big dreams, cross the seas, and build something grand from your dreams. If all men chose to pray on their knees, day after day and month after month, like monks in a monastery, the Great Wall of China would have never been built and no man would have landed on the moon and planted an American flag. Then, the world we live in would be a boring place. I respect your father. He lived as a Jesuit, yet he was human in his heart and in his mind. He wasn't a robot made of plastic."

Michael told him about a letter his father had written him, which he had found in the box, along with other belongings, including diaries, which Father Murphy had kept in his office for more than three decades. "After reading the letter to me, apologizing for neglecting me and severing his relationship with my mother for the sake of his reputation as the dean of the College, I feel that he might have planned for his death. But Father Patrick didn't think so. What's your opinion on that, Coach?"

Wong had a mysterious grin spreading on his face. "I believe a man should be able to choose when or how he should end his life. Beyond that, I have nothing more to say."

"How long did you talk to him that day?"

"About an hour or more," he said, his eyes glued to the windshield. "He unexpectedly stopped the van in a wooded area on the shoulder of the highway and said he'd like to be alone, apologizing for not taking me back to the College. The sky had turned gray and rain began to spatter on the windshield.

"I said, 'No problem,' but wasn't glad when I had to walk five miles to the nearest bus station. The next thing I knew, he'd drowned."

Chapter Seventeen
Brainstorming for the Task

"I want to talk to you about what to expect in the North," Min began one morning to the group. "Everything we've talked about inside these walls is very important, but what we're going to discuss today is even more important, because we're actually exploring *life* in the North: who awaits us, how North Koreans see us, and what to expect from them. In other words, see yourselves through North Koreans' eyes. There're two kinds of people in the North—the predators and the prey. Secret agents are always looking for what they call 'enemies of the Democratic People's Republic of Korea' and are ready to crack your heads open at any given moment. The rest of the people are living in fear, fear that anyone looking at them could be secret police and they try to avoid any attention. Any questions?"

When no one raised their hand, he went on: "My advice to you is don't ask unnecessary questions. You might not realize this, but at an unexpected moment, you might speak with Southern accent, and that can be a potential noose that'll choke the *life* out of you. It's similar to identifying yourself as an enemy."

Needle Doctor said, "I'm from Busan and I still have a Southern accent when I'm not careful, though I lived in Seoul for more than 30 years. What should I do?"

"Be careful, by all means!" Min said, nailing each word. "Peter the Apostle said, 'Be watchful. Your adversary the devil prowls around like a roaring lion, seeking someone to devour.' Remember that?"

"I'm fine most of the time," Needle Doctor said. "But when I'm extremely tired, I don't know what comes out of my mouth—my southern dialect or Chinese."

"I have an advice for you," Min said. "Don't bother North Koreans you don't know, and they won't bother you. In fact, they're so afraid they avoid eye-contact with *anyone*."

"Yes, Boss."

"I have a question for everyone," Min continued. "During our rest stops in small eateries or at a public bathroom, someone might approach you and say he or she wants to go to the South with you. What will you do?"

"I'll keep my mouth shut," the Whistle-blower said.

"Why?"

"Because that person might be a plainclothes secret agent trying to trick me."

"No. Tell him or her to come see me," Min said.

"I thought you said 'safety first' earlier."

"I know, but we don't want to scare away anyone who wants to defect to the South. Those who approach us might have seen some of us during our earlier missions and gathered courage to ask, risking their necks. And remember, there're rewards for secret agents and patrol guards to report any potential enemy of the Democratic People's Republic of Korea. It's a tricky business to balance your safety and helping potential defectors. All you can do is keep your eyes and ears open and do your best."

"Yes, Boss."

Coach volunteered. "There are exceptions, guys. Once, here in Seoul, I interviewed two defectors who escaped the North together. One was a security officer on border patrol duty and the other was his prisoner, caught while crawling under an electric fence in an escape attempt. According to the former guard, his young prisoner, barely 18 years old, persuaded him to leave the regime with him. They both crawled under an electric barbed-wire fence in early dawn and ran across a field until they reached Dandong, a town on the border between China and North Korea, where many of our friends live and we're heading in a few days. That 32-year-old guard had been planning to defect to the South for some time, and when he heard the young prisoner's determined plea to escape the regime, he made up his mind to go with him. In this business, you never know what you might run into, but God certainly will be there with you. Any questions?"

130

When no one said anything, Min concluded the meeting, saying, "Have good dreams, brothers. We leave in one week."

Michael accepted the idea of going to North Korea with Min's group for two purposes: to deliver Bibles to North Koreans and help some brave souls wanting to defect to the South but he didn't feel ready for such a challenging trip within a week. Before he came to Korea three years earlier, he had lived in Texas as an aimless youth full of doubts about his future. He didn't know anything about his birthparents. He frequently thought of Max, the boy two years older who had given him the courage to run away with him from the farmhouse to a vacant home in the woods, where the two of them had a great time until they met Bob and Jimmy—the drug dealers who got them in trouble with the law.

Now, as a grown man living in Korea, he was a murder suspect sought by the police, who was about to leave for North Korea to deliver Bibles to North Korean Christians, knowing that the borders were highly militarized, with minefields, checkpoints, and barbed-wire fences. He couldn't believe how turbulent his life had been, nor did he know what future was waiting for him. He had a humble wish: *I want to come back; I don't want to live there,* he thought.

Chapter Eighteen
Emergency Drill

The next morning, a call from the Korean Coastal Guards alerted the six men with unexpected news: a passenger ship carrying more than 100 passengers from Ulleung Island near the west coast, mostly seafood merchants heading to Seoul, was sinking 1,500 meters from its destination from engine problems. "They need our help!" Min said.

"Wait, we're not coastal guards," Michael pointed out. "And we're not trained for sea rescue."

"What difference does it make?" Coach said. "We trained you to save others. It will be a good opportunity to use our skills in a real situation. Get moving!"

The team, dressed in Emergency Rescue Uniforms, was waiting on the hill behind the boarding school when an American helicopter with red, blue, and white painted on its body appeared from the southern side. It landed 50 feet away, its giant blades still whipping. The men ran and boarded. It lifted effortlessly into the air and flew east. In less than 15 minutes, Michael looked down at a white boat lying on its side, surrounded by tiny dots that appeared to be the passengers trying to save themselves. The wind was icy cold. As the helicopter descended, people in the water seemed more desperate than Michael had thought earlier—some swam towards the shore, some merely bobbed in the water, and some barely hung onto the sinking boat. Two identical red boats bearing 'Coastal Security Rescue' on their sides were approaching the sinking ship. Without a warning, Coach ordered, "Ready? Jump!" They landed in the water with a loud splash.

Michael was nervous. His Emergency Rescue Uniform was heavy and bulky. And he was cold. Yet, men and women hanging onto the boat and crying 'Help, help!' gave him no time to worry about his own discomfort. An old man with a balding head about 20 feet away from where he just landed caught his attention. Eyes closed, the old man was meekly floating in water in the helicopter's light, his head bobbing on the surface.

Michael swam to him. "I'm here to help you, sir," he said, and the old man opened his eyes and nodded, spewing water from his mouth. Reaching for him cautiously, Michael grabbed the back of his tweed topcoat with one hand and swam with his free arm towards one of the rescue boats anchored about 100 feet away. As they approached, the boat captain threw an air tube tied to a rope towards them and Michael caught it. He placed it around the old man's midsection and waved to the captain. He then watched the old man gliding on the water and the captain and two other men pulling him up like two fishermen reeling in a giant fish they had just caught. With a sense of relief, Michael threw his arms into the air and the crew waved back.

That was easy, Michael thought. A sense of gladness came over him, knowing the old man would live because of his help. Others in his team were helping women and children clinging onto the boat, splashing at the same time. Michael dove deep into the water to find someone who might have slipped away unnoticed. The water under the boat was so murky that he couldn't see anything. Then, something caught his attention— the propeller was still turning. A sickening feeling came over him when he noticed something red turning with the blades. He got closer and saw that it was a small boy wearing a red overall, caught by one of the turning blades. *What happened to the parents?*

He approached the propeller carefully. The boy seemed lifeless. Unless he disabled the motor, this tiny corpse would never be discovered. He took a deep breath and sank deeper into the water in hopes of touching the seafloor with his feet so that he would have better leverage on it. Then it happened; he was on his feet on the soft sand. The magic of gravity! It was a great feeling. Then, something sharp and heavy stabbed the left side of his head. *The blade!* In dismay, he found himself gliding

133

away. *Am I dying*? he thought. The current carried him effortlessly and he was very tired. *Someone please help me!*

A hand grabbed one of his arms and then the other arm and he was lifted. Men were talking. He was completely awake, yet his arms and legs felt wobbly and numb. He was aware that he was being taken to the rescue boat, maybe the same rescue boat he himself had taken the old man to only minutes earlier. He felt safe.

Men's voices woke him. He found himself flat on his back, with the strong smell of alcohol around him. His eyelids were heavy.

"He can't travel in this condition!" a man's voice said with authority.

"Then we can delay our departure a few days," another voice answered. It was a familiar voice. *Reverend Min, the boss?*

"A few days?" the first man's voice said. "He lost a great deal of blood and one side of his skull is split open. He needs treatments that can take upto three weeks at least."

He must be my doctor, Michael decided.

"Three weeks!" Min said. "We have to leave in ten days. Is there any possibility he can be released sooner?"

"No!" the doctor said. "He'll be lucky if he's fully recovered after three weeks. Sometimes an infection settles in, complicating things. But ten days is out of the question."

Michael heard diminishing footsteps on the floor, followed by a door closing. A sharp pain throbbed in his left temple and at the same time bright lights flashed in his eyes. Michael heard himself moaning.

"Michael. Are you alright?"

It was Min's voice. "I am not, Boss. Where am I?"

"In a hospital the coastguards took you. Get some sleep. I'll come see you tomorrow."

After Min left, Michael felt confused. He couldn't figure out why he was lying there or why the two men had been arguing about how long he'd stay in the hospital. He was thirsty too. Mostly he felt as if he were in another world, in a white world where everything floated in the air. His eyelids were heavy and he felt he was drifting somewhere, like a speck of dust.

Chapter Nineteen
His Father's Grave

The day he was released from the hospital, Michael asked Reverend Min if he could stay with Father Patrick for a couple of days before the team embarked for the North. Min had no objections to that. In fact, he called Father Patrick and asked for his approval and even drove Michael to Sochun Catholic Church.

The two religious leaders shook hands amicably before Min departed, with Father Patrick's promise to bring Michael to their gathering place, the boarding school, in two days.

"Welcome back, Michael," Father Patrick said in his usual warm voice and embraced him.

"Thank you, Father, for accommodating me. Staying here with you a couple of days will help me to get better sooner."

"I'm glad you chose that option, but you want to visit your father's grave, I believe, before your departure. I was informed about your mission to the North by Dr. Kim."

"Dr. Kim? How does he know I've joined the group helping North Koreans?"

"It's a small world, Michael. He and Min were in Vietnam at the same time."

"I didn't know that!"

As they passed the church and headed for the rectory, Michael found himself talking to his father. *Father, I can't leave for North Korea without touching the soil that covers you. Please, guide me and share your wisdom and courage that brought you to Korea half century earlier. I need it.*

Inside his office, Father Patrick said, "I want you to take the next room, my bedroom, because the bed is more comfortable than this sofa."

"No, Father, I'll sleep here tonight."

The secretary, Mrs. Hahn, emerged from the next room. "Father, he's a young man," she said. "He can sleep anywhere, and that sofa is plenty comfortable for anyone. And he slept on it before."

Michael was about to agree with her, but Father Patrick dismissed her, saying, "We can use some hot tea, Mrs. Hahn. And cancel all my appointments this afternoon. Thank you."

She looked at Father Patrick as if she had something to say, but when Father Patrick ignored her, she quickly left.

Michael knew why Mrs. Hahn wasn't glad to see him. To her, he was the thief who stole her employer's new black suit and his briefcase and vanished. *Did she read the newspapers that described me as a kidnap-murder suspect sought by the police?*

Father Patrick opened the door connecting to his bedroom and invited Michael in. While Michael stood and watched, he removed the bedsheet and pillowcases from his bed and opened the closet to find a new set of sheets and pillowcases.

Michael said, "Father, I never apologized for taking your black suit and briefcase without asking. I was a thief."

"You don't need to apologize for anything, Michael," he said, without turning to look at him. "Actually, I'm glad that you took my suit because the sleeves were too long for me."

Michael couldn't help but laugh. "I'll pay you back some day."

"You don't need to." He finally turned to him, with a new set of bedsheets. "Let me tell you something I've never told anyone. Shortly after I joined the Sonam College faculty in 1965, I wrecked your father's van in an accident, injuring myself too. Your father was pretty upset for the damage I caused to the van that belonged to the College, but he never mentioned it to me. Compared to what I did to him, you taking my suit is nothing. Don't worry about it."

He then resumed covering the bed with the new set of sheets.

"Father, what you did was an accident. But I premeditated my crime. There's no excuse."

A quizzical smile spread across Father Patrick's face. "You have a valid point there, Michael. In that case, get me a new pair of sneakers instead of replacing my black suit. My old sneakers have holes in the soles. Nothing lasts forever."

After lunch break, they walked to his father's grave on the hill behind the Administration building. It was the way Michael had imagined—yet very different. The entire cemetery lot was the size of the auditorium, bordered with tall prairie grasses swaying in the gentle wind. To his surprise, the graves were smooth, round mounds, the same as all Korean people's graves.

Father Patrick led Michael to a middle row of the mounds, stopping in front of a headstone. "Here, Michael. This is your father's burial spot."

Michael read the inscription on the granite headpiece. *First dean and founder of Sonam College, Father John Dolan, SJ, rests here. His Jesuit vision and spirit are the roots to this ever-growing first adult-education center in the heart of Seoul. 'I am the light of the world. Whoever follows me will not walk in darkness, but will have the light of life.' John 8:12.*

Michael knelt before the headstone, and soon he found himself crying. Father Patrick sat next to him without uttering a sound. Michael had many things to tell his father, whom he had never seen, yet words seemed powerless. Still, he knew his father was watching him from Heaven above. Somewhere, a magpie was trilling in its clear voice and Michel thought his father's spirit was trying to tell him something.

Chapter Twenty
Journey to the Unknown

A few days before Christmas, Reverend Min told the team to pack each of their rucksacks with 25 Bibles and cross-pendants, warm clothes, food, toiletries, and multiple vitamins. "We're leaving tonight," he said, throwing a quick glance in Michael's direction on his left. "Every Bible we carry on our back will protect us, but we should never underestimate Satan's power to push us away from our Master. Are you with Him?"

"Yes, boss!"

"Good! One more thing; as we've talked about, when you're caught, do not reveal any information about the group. Our friendly North Koreans will do everything to help us escape, but there's no guarantee. Once caught, the secret police will force you to admit that you have been conducting hostile acts against the DPRK or tried to set up underground activist groups somewhere to topple what they call their 'Great Nation'. Don't ever argue with them. Admit it and apologize. Otherwise you'll be tortured or poisoned with toxic chemicals."

It was a long day for Michael. His recent medical trauma made him ill-prepared for the trip, carrying his backpack with two dozen Bibles and other things. He was also nostalgic about leaving Seoul. Here in this ancient town, he had performed with his band more than a hundred times; he had met Father Patrick for the first time and learned of his father and connected with his mother too, whom he unexpectedly lost in a boat accident. Now, he was leaving, not knowing when he'd return. *Will I come back?*

That evening, after a simple meal, they walked up to the spot near the pond where they had been training for this trip during the past three weeks and waited for their ride. The scene was spectacular, with the reflection of the setting sun on the surface of the pond on one side and a broad view of the horizon down below on the other, with miniature cars and trucks racing on the highways, jungles of tall buildings, and homes of all sizes. Two bright headlights climbed up from behind a hill and approached them. The car honked as it stopped before the team. Up close, it was a military jeep with two extended seats in the rear. The driver was a young soldier with a solemn face.

With a quick arm's motion, Rev. Min ordered the team to board the jeep. Michael took the seat behind the driver. The driver looked at Michael for a long moment through the rear view mirror as if he recognized him. But, Michael pretended he didn't notice and got busy setting his backpack on the floor and buckling his seatbelt.

"Welcome aboard," the driver said, without turning. "I'm your guide, assigned to drive you to Sokcho on the east coast. I just received a message from headquarters that you'll depart Sokcho tomorrow afternoon and spend tonight in the private home of a Vietnam vet who is an ardent supporter of this mission." Everyone looked at one another, trying to figure out who could be their ardent supporter of their mission and why they hadn't been informed earlier.

"Did you know about this, Boss?" someone asked.

Min replied, "No, but we'll find out soon!"

With a loud 'Brrrrm', the jeep lurched forwards and darted towards the mountains ahead. Clouds behind the mountains were stained pink and lavender by the setting sun.

* * *

Rustling noises woke Michael. Everyone was piling off the jeep, each carrying his backpack. A large traditional Korean-style structure with a curvy roofline stood in front of him, under the dark sky dotted with hundreds of stars. *Why are we here?* he wondered.

"Michael, get out!" Coach yelled. "We're staying here tonight, remember?"

He remembered. They had just arrived at the 'private home' the driver had mentioned. This place was brightly lit, surrounded by tall, straight pines. He got out of the car and followed Coach to the building. He saw a poster, 'Vietnam War

Veterans' Christmas Party' on the door. He suddenly felt a pang of hunger. A shaft of bright light descended through a stairwell, showing their way to an upper floor.

At the landing upstairs, he saw a large room decorated with Santa's jolly faces and a tall, brightly lit Christmas tree in the center. Several tables loaded with food around the tree greeted them. A few women wearing white aprons over their Korean dresses busily moved about—some bringing platters and loading them onto the tables and others rearranging plates and bowls, making noise. Here and there, a few soldiers and men in civilian clothes stood and talking, some holding drinks.

A soldier in his 50s walked up to Coach, shook hands with him, and the two chatted in a friendly manner. The soldier looked familiar to Michael but he couldn't remember where he might have met him. Coach turned to Michael as if to introduce him to the soldier, but the soldier spoke first, "Hey, Michael, so glad to see you! I've heard that you joined us."

Us? "Pardon me, sir, but I can't remember where I've met you!"

The soldier laughed. "I'm Dr. Kim."

"Dr. Kim!" Michael cried in glee. "I'm sorry… I didn't recognize you. You look different in that military uniform."

"Do I look better in this or worse?

"You look great always."

Kim laughed. "I'm glad you're here!"

"But where am I, Dr. Kim? I thought we were heading to the North via Dandong, China, and the driver informed us that we'd stop at a private home. This doesn't look like a private home to me."

"It was my idea, Michael," Kim said in a militaristic way. "And this is the home I share with my partner, Yim, you met at the cabin. The reason we kept quiet about our party was for safety. There are many North Korean agents disguised as defectors who can spoil things in many ways, besides kidnapping and murdering innocent people."

"You and Mr. Yim own this home?" Michael asked in disbelief.

"Yes. We've been using this home for our monthly Vietnam War Veterans meeting and also holiday gatherings for a few years. But this year, we added the foot soldiers working in the North to our guest list."

Michael was a bit uncomfortable for being identified as *a foot soldier working in the North.* "This is my first time going to North Korea."

"I know it! You'll do well, Michael. Reverend Min is also a Vietnam War Veteran. He said positive things about you."

"He did?"

"Yes! Many times. Come. I'll show you the place."

Dr. Kim led him out of the room with the tables loaded with food where soldiers and civilians mingled together and entered the next room. It was a larger room with a pool table in the middle and a stage in the corner with a few chairs, music stands, a drum, and a guitar stand—as if a band would soon perform. In the opposite corner stood a bar where a man sat on one of the tall stools and was drinking alone.

Seeing the stage setup for a band performance made Michael melancholy about his performing days as a band musician. He missed his six band members, as well as his guitar. *What happened to my guitar?* It'd only been a month since he had stopped singing and playing his guitar, but it seemed longer. Sometimes, when he wasn't aware, his left fingers raced on his imaginary guitar-fingerboard aimlessly. *Where are the guys today? Are they still giving the weekly concert at the New Age Theater?* "What band is playing tonight?" Michael asked Dr. Kim.

"I'm not sure. We have different groups coming each time."

A black musician in a black tuxedo, holding a clarinet, walked onto the stage and tested the microphone by tapping it gently. Michael was alert. Something about him was familiar. And this musician was holding the clarinet the way Charlie used to, in his left hand, while he did other things with his right hand. At the possibility of seeing Charlie, his heart ached with longing. Michael said to Dr. Kim, "I want to talk to that musician for a while, Dr. Kim. We used to play together."

"Very well. I'll see you later, Michael. I'll be around!"

When Dr. Kim left, he ran to the stage calling, "Hey, Charlie!"

Charlie froze for a moment, and then his dark face bloomed into a wide smile, his white teeth showing. "Hey, buddy, I can't believe this!" They hugged.

At Michael's suggestion, they moved to the bar and ordered a beer each. Two beer bottles arrived at no time and they clinked and wished one another best. After a sip, Charlie said, "I read about you in the paper but I didn't believe a word I read. It was bullshit!"

A sigh escaped Michael's throat. "It's a long story, Charlie," he said, sensing a pain in his gut. "All I can say is, I don't regret what I did. Mother didn't want to be kept alive in that cancer clinic by a ventilator and oxygen machine."

"I'm with you 100% on that, Michael. God in Heaven will crown you for what you did, I'm sure. Hey, I have something to tell you."

"What?"

"I found my Dad!" Charlie said and laughed bashfully, like a child.

"You found who?"

"Actually, he found me. Out of the blue, I got a call from the U.S. Embassy here in Seoul, shortly after I last saw you. Remember the night a gang of Korean urchins beat me?"

"I sure do!"

"At first, I thought someone called the wrong number and hung up. I never dreamt that someone at the U.S. Embassy would call me. The phone rang again, and when I picked it up, it was the same guy. This time, he introduced himself as Kent Morrison and asked me if I were Charlie Knox, pronouncing my name slowly and clearly. I said yes, and he asked whether I was born in Seoul and lived in St. Agatha Catholic Orphanage until I was adopted to the Knox family in Chicago, giving some dates. When I said yes to all he asked, he told me to go to a testing lab near my house in Shinchon and follow the instructions. 'We'll talk soon,' he said and hung up the phone.

"Three days later, Morrison called again. 'Mr. Knox, would you come to the Embassy tomorrow morning? We have a very important issue to discuss with you. We open at nine in the morning.' I got there shortly after they opened the door. The receptionist called Morrison and he came to get me. He was a tall, lanky American, a perfect type to be a diplomat. He took me to his office, where an old black couple sat together on the sofa. 'Mr. and Mrs. Knox,' Morrison said. 'This gentleman here is the man you've been searching for years. His DNA proved that he's your son, Mr. Knox!' The old man started to cry as I stood there mutely, not believing what I just heard."

"You mean, you didn't say anything to your dad?" Michael asked.

"At first, no. My mind was blank. Strangely, though, I found the old man somewhat familiar. The black lady next to him must have read my mind. She said, 'God heard our prayers, Daniel,' touching the crying man's elbow. 'You two look so much alike!' She then cried covering her face with her hands. Can you believe such a thing can happen to a 26-year-old guy?"

Michael threw his arms around Charlie and held him tight. "I'm happy for you, Charlie. The night you handed me that white notepaper with the hand-scribbled note after our concert, I didn't know what to think. But now I'm a different guy. Thank you, Charlie, for giving me that note from Father Patrick!"

"Hey, I was very happy that night. Remember? I danced for you! Anyway, I asked them how they found me and why, after all these years, and Dad told me everything. He said that after he learned of his lung cancer three years ago, he went through some inner turmoil. One night, he told his wife about his illegitimate son born of a Korean woman he had a brief relationship with, and she was shocked, he said. She scolded him, calling him a heartless brute. She began to search for me through the Internet, without even knowing my name or anything. But, my Dad had a pretty good memory about when I was born and where my birthmother lived, eventually matching me with the orphanage where I was taken by a Catholic nun. I guess there weren't too many black infants born during the war and abandoned later by their Korean mothers."

Their conversation was disrupted by the band director, a Korean man who rushed over, saying, "Clarinet! What are you doing? We are about to begin. Hurry!"

Charlie ran to the stage with the conductor, unable to say anything to Michael, and within seconds, the band played the Korean national anthem and everyone rose to their feet and sang.

143

Though the Eastern Sea might dry out someday
and Baekdu Mountain might be flattened,
God the Almighty will never stop protecting our nation.
Our national flower, Hibiscus, blooming everywhere in
spring,
We shall live happily together forever and ever.

The program began with Dr. Kim's introductions. In his army uniform, under the bright stage light, Dr. Kim looked taller and all capable as he spoke: "Fellow Koreans, we've gathered here tonight to celebrate our fellowship and to reaffirm our obligation towards our North Korean brothers suffering in Kim Jong-il's regime. Our guest speaker tonight is Reverend Hahn, an American citizen and a Presbyterian minister who made hundreds of trips to North Korea, delivering the good news of Jesus Christ. But he was captured four years ago and endured back-breaking labor in a prison camp along the Yalu River. He escaped with the help of our devout Christian friends, along with thousands of others. Tonight, he'll shed light on your journey to the North by sharing his own experience there."

Dr. Kim clapped his hands vigorously as an old man in a gray suit and black tie walked onto the stage and bowed deeply in the traditional Korean manner. The clapping stopped as the old man faced them.

Hahn thanked Dr. Kim briefly, with a nod, and opened a paper and read from it. "Dear friends in Christ. I sincerely hope that what I'm about to say will help you on your journey to North Korea tomorrow, whether it's your 1st time or 25th. Each of us is called to do what our Master Jesus commanded us to do: '*Whatever you did for one of the least of your brothers, you did for Me*'."

Loud applause rose in the room but quickly died down as he continued. "I have been in the North 156 times before I was captured by a young North Korean guard on border duty. It was after I intentionally left a Bible in the men's bathroom. I was hunted down and caught 50 miles away from where I left the Bible. Do you know why they hate anyone leaving the Bible in such a public place? Behind their fear of the Bible is their guilt for having abandoned Christ and having been worshipping the

144

wrong man, their deity Kim Jong-il. Once upon a time, North Korea had many Christian churches, Christian schools, and missionaries from all over the world. Do you know how many North Koreans have defected to the South in recent years? Twenty thousand in less than 10 years, but the numbers are growing. And you're aware that many North Korean secret agents are sent to the South to destroy those who left Kim's regime. They use poison sprays, pills, pens, and torch guns to kill soundlessly. Often, high school and college students are terrorists, trained in a four-year espionage school. They are skilled in martial arts, scuba diving, shooting, and handling explosives and poison weapons."

The audience was deadly silent.

"The fundamental rule since ancient Korea is still practiced in the North—*kill, if not, you'll be killed!* The spies are ordered to kill themselves when their missions are botched. One spy I know who couldn't kill himself, because he lost consciousness when he was shot, woke up in a South Korean military hospital hours later. Soon after, North Korean military intelligence killed all of his family members and close relatives in the North as punishment for him not having fulfilled his duties as a spy. Shortly, he too was murdered by poison chemicals, here in Seoul. This shows that the South Korean security system isn't completely reliable, and we try our best to conceal important gatherings, such as this party tonight, from all possible dangers. In short, North Korean leaders had turned away from God's merciful love a long time ago and have become Satan followers. That's why North Koreans need each of us. We're God's messengers. Although I vowed never to step on North Korean soil after I escaped, I have done so many times, knowing I can be captured again and die there. My belief is that whatever I do for our North Korean brothers and sisters pleases God. What more do I want as His servant? May God bless you all!" Rousing applause again filled the room.

A group of men and women in identical uniforms walked up to the stage and posed for the next program. Dr. Kim announced that a mixed voice choir from the Seoul University School of Music was about to sing Beethoven's choral music '*Ode to Joy*'.

To Michael's surprise, the conductor was a young woman dressed in a black tuxedo. With a deep bow to the audience, she turned to the choir and began waving her baton energetically above her head, as if she had done it all her life, and the choir sang the first verse with piano accompaniment. The conductor unexpectedly turned and motioned to the audience to join the choir. Noises of chairs moving against the hard floor followed. Then, everyone stood and sang:

Joyful, joyful, we adore Thee, God of glory, Lord of love;
Hearts unfold like flowers before Thee, opening to the sun above.
Melt the clouds of sin and sadness; drive the dark of doubt away;
Giver of immortal gladness, fill us with the light of day!
All Thy works with joy surround Thee, earth and heaven reflect Thy rays,
Stars and angels sing around Thee, center of unbroken praise.
Field and forest, vale and mountain, flowery meadow, flashing sea,
Singing bird and flowing fountain call us to rejoice in Thee.

It was uplifting for Michael as he sang this solemn hymn, which was the last movement of Beethoven's Chorale Symphony. The melody was simple, yet the words spoke to him with power. When the singing ended, the stage was cleared quickly and Reverend Min took the podium. Pausing a moment, he began to read from the Bible:

"Therefore I tell you, brethren, do not worry about your life, what you will eat or drink; or about your body, what you will wear. Is not life more than food, and the body more than clothes? Look at the birds of the air: They do not sow or reap or gather into barns—and yet your Heavenly Father feeds them. Are you not much more valuable than they? Who of you by worrying can add a single hour to his lifespan?"

Min closed the Bible and looked at the audience before he spoke. "Dear brothers, I'm privileged and honored to deliver

146

God's message that He'll be with you on your journey to the North, according to Luke 12-verses 22 to 34. Those are the words of God himself. I hereby give you His blessing; in the name of the Father, Son, and the Holy Spirit. Go in peace!"

Everyone, soldiers and civilians alike, rose to their feet and lowered their heads in solemnity and prayed. After Reverend Min walked down the stage, Dr. Kim reappeared and lifted his arms wide and said, "Brothers, thank you for making this evening memorable. Merry Christmas!"

Michael didn't move as Reverend Min's voice still rang in his ears: '*Do not worry about your life, what you will eat or drink; or about your body, what you will wear. Is not life more than food, and the body more than clothes...?*' Gradually, the voice changed to his father's, which he had never heard in his entire life but he knew. '*Look at the birds of the air... They do not sow or reap or gather into barns—and yet your Heavenly Father feeds them. Michael, trust Him. Are you not much more valuable than the birds in the air?*'

The End

CPSIA information can be obtained
at www.ICGtesting.com
Printed in the USA
BVHW041054280719
554512BV00021B/853/P